Dust Covered Memories

Tom Power

First Published in 2015
Printed by Modern Printers, Kilkenny
Tel: 056 7721739

ISBN: 978-0-9557054-2-7

Dust Covered Memories

Chapter One

...and when we are older we will think of our youth,
spend searching for pleasure and seeking the truth...

My name is Jim Clarke. I'm on holidays in Ireland, a nice
break from the hustle and bustle of London. I'm staying
with my aunt, Helen Flynn and her son Paul near a quiet
village a few miles from Waterford city. Paul is in his
mid thirties and is a typical Irish bachelor, still living at
home. Though to be fair to Paul his father died about
five years ago and he said he had to postpone moving
out. We are having an enjoyable night in the pub, a
large crowd, good craic; and a sing song.
Paul said "it's nice to see such a large crowd here, since
the collapse of the economy, and with thousands of
young people emigrating many pubs have closed, but

now things are starting to pick up again."

"I think Paul in some ways Ireland has changed a lot and in more ways something's never change."

"True Jim, our beliefs on religion, divorce and contraception has changed big time. I suppose the sex scandals in the church have changed our way of thinking, and yet as far as unemployment is concerned we're much the same as we were sixty or seventy years ago."

"I know Paul, that's hard to believe, and mass emigration still a curse. I suppose you could say all brands of politicians have let us down."

"I often ask myself the question Jim, are we capable of self government?"

"My advice to you Paul is... if you want a peaceful life; make sure it's only yourself you ask that question to."

I ordered another two pints and said, "Now let's forget about the unemployment, emigration, religion and everything else, and enjoy the craic and worry about the headache in the morning."

The musicians finished playing a few tunes. Then the M C called on someone called Ted to sing. I turned around to see who it was.

A man with grey hair was sitting in the corner. I guessed his age to be about sixty. The M C called for silence and said, "Come on Ted, oblige us." Ted cleared his throat,

took a swig of his Guinness and started to sing. I
switched on the recorder on my mobile phone, even
though the reception was bad it might pick up some of
the words. He wasn't a bad singer, but it was the words
of his song that held my attention more so than his
voice. I listened as he sang.

*She was a poet in her teens, her pen just wrote down the
truth / but the truth is often ignored, they called her a
pot smoking youth / They put her down as a beatnik;
well she did wear a flower in her hair / maybe she was a
bit of beat, but in her heart she really did care.*

I thought the words beatnik, flowers in her hair and
pot, clearly placed this song in the sixties. I listened as
Ted continued. He sang of the Vietnam War, Apartheid,
of trouble in Ulster; J F K, and Martin Luther King. He
sang of bar stools in Chelsea, busking in Hampstead, a
walk on the heath; a park bench in Highgate, and
returning to Ireland. And years later she becomes a
famous author. And bringing it into the present with
these lines

*Now in the Twenty First Century you youth of the world
have your say / try and persuade all our leaders that
peace not war is the way.*

And finishing off with,

3

As I went to the bookshop that evening I thought she now has the world at her feet / as I flicked the fly leaf I read, to a friend for the night we walked over the heath.

I was intrigued with Ted's song. It was more of a story than a song, originating in the sixties and ending in the present day. I made a mental note to speak to him and clapped along with the rest when he finished.
I said to Paul, "I never heard that song before."
"I've heard Ted sing it a few times Jim."
"I must ask him about it."
"Why?"
"I think it's a great song, it's got history attached to it, a virtual list of all the important events of the sixties, and it surely has the makings of a good story."
"I know you're a journalist Jim and you've had a few short stories published, but do you really think you can get a story from an old man singing a song."
"I think it just might be worth pursuing, if I can get more information about the song and on whoever wrote it, there might be a story there."

Paul called Ted over. "Ted this is my cousin Jim, he's a journalist working with some paper in London and he is intrigued with that song you just sang. He thinks he could get a good story from it."
I shook hands with him and said, "That song was great,

a wonderful story with a beginning, middle and an end."
Ted said "I'm glad you like it, but it wasn't always a
song, it started life as a poem. I put a bit of a tune to it,
and I think every song should have a beginning, middle
and an end."
"Well that one certainly has, it starts in the sixties and
ends in the present day."
"So you're a journalist, are you in Fleet Street?"
"No, no, nothing like that, I'm working for a weekly
tabloid called *Here and There* it covers events in Ireland
and England that are of interest to the Irish in England."
"I use to work in Fleet Street, on the printing presses in
the sixties."
"It's all changed now Ted, all digital, and those big
printing presses all obsolete."
"I guess that's progress, the world forever developing
and changing, it's hard to keep up with it all" Ted said.

A woman shouted at Ted from the doorway.
Ted stood up and said, "I'm sorry, I have to go. My lift
home has arrived, but if you're in tomorrow night we
can talk more about it."
"Grand I'd love to, yes I'll be here."
"Good until tomorrow night, good night then."

"I wasn't expecting to hear all those places in London
mentioned here Paul, *in the* back *of beyond.*

"Now Jim, don't put us down, maybe we are living *in the back of beyond*, but it's our choice to live here, it's a nice easy way of life."

"I know, I know, sorry, it's grand here and I enjoy coming over for a quiet break, away from the helter skelter of the city. What's his second name?"

"Who's second name?"

"Ted's second name."

"Patterson... Patterson, he's been living here for over twenty years now, he lived in England many years ago, and I think he's been to Australia and America, so it's not so surprising that he knows all those places in London."

"I'm looking forward to talking to him. I'm sure there's a story in that song."

"All may be revealed tomorrow night, it will be quiet here, and the few young lads that haven't emigrated will be gone to town clubbing, ye can talk away to your hearts content." The M C called on Paul for a song. Paul declined and said, "Not tonight."

Chapter Two

Saturday morning, Paul and I were out early, trying to walk away our headache after the excess of the night before. We walked through the village down to the lake and along the lakeside path. Two swans were motionless in the water, a water hen, followed by her clutch swam westward across the lake, creating an ever increasing ripple that would make landfall on the north, and south bank.

I said to Paul, "Do you think Ted will be in the pub tonight?"
"He said he would Jim, so I'm sure he will."
"I'm looking forward to hearing about that song."
"It's only another song, why are you so interested in it."
"That's the point, I don't think it's just another song, I think it's got a story behind it, and I think Ted know that story."
"If there is a story, are you sure he will want to tell it."
"There's a story alright, and if not, maybe something for my paper. I switched on my recorder; but with the bad reception and the noise of the pub it had only picked up some of the words. Just listen; these words surely have a story of some kind attached to them."

I remember the first day... she said peace not war... in Chelsea debating who shot J F K... her one day in Hampstead busking... on the street... to a cafe for coffee... walked over the heath... a park bench in Highgate, and talked...I convinced to continue... it's the book of the year... the world at her feet...

"Convinced who to continue what? And book of the year? She must be someone famous. There's a story Paul, but who is it about? Who has the world at their feet? Is it some worldwide celebrity that we all know and is Ted willing to tell it or not? Let's wait and see."
"And if he is willing to tell it, will he give you the true version Jim, or the version that suits him?"

On our way back through the Village Paul bought one of the local weekly papers, and a daily paper; then it was back to Paul's house for a full Irish breakfast, prepared by his mother.
She said, "It was the best cure for a hangover, and as she didn't have one, she would have the breakfast enjoyed by the ancients, porridge and honey".
During breakfast I told Helen about Ted's song, and that I was intrigued by both him and the song. I asked her, "What part of England was he in?"
"I'm almost sure it was London. He came to live here about twenty years ago, he lives on his own; he used to

work in Waterford Institute of Technology, as a printer I think, and is now retired."

"Has he had any girl friends in his life?"

"A few on and off through the years, none lasted too long."

"And the woman who drove him home last night?"

"That's his neighbour, Biddy Murphy; she drives him for a few pints now and then, like all rural dwellers, the drink - driving laws have affected him. Often when I pick up Paul I give Ted a lift home as well."

"Has he a car?"

"He has... not of much use to him when he wants to go for a pint. He has the free bus pass as well, only one problem there... no buses. He lives a quiet life, he walks and reads, drinks a few pints in the local pub. In the summer he walks to the pub, but in the winter, he has to depend on other people. Since he came here I don't think he's ever left... oh sorry yes, last year he was away for about a week. I don't think you could call Ted intriguing."

"Maybe not Helen, but I think the song is and I would like to talk to him about it."

"Your father and mother are good I hope. Are they coming over this year?"

"They're great, father working hard, they go to the Irish centre at the weekend, a few drinks and a dance. No they're not coming this year, they're going to Portugal, they're hoping you might visit them; you haven't been over for years."

"I know the last time I was over Jack came with me, God be good to him. I'll think about it, maybe I'll visit sometime this year."

I read the two papers that Paul had bought, and then had a wash and shave. The afternoon and evening passed quickly enough, and at nine o' clock Paul and I were walking to the village.

Helen said "Give me a call when ye are ready to come home."

As Paul had predicted, the pub was quiet, apart from an over abundance of televisions that needed turning down, or preferably turning off. The young people had gone clubbing to the city. We sat at the counter and ordered a couple of pints. There were about six or seven people in the bar, all older than us. Then the door opened, and in walked Ted.

He came over to join us, sat on a barstool next to me, nodded, and said hello to Paul, and ordered a pint.

"You must be Theresa's son then" he said.

"I am."

"My! It seems like only yesterday you were a child coming here on holidays with her, time flies, and the older you get the quicker it goes."

"You knew my mother?"

"Not really, I know of her coming over for holidays now and then, she is a good bit younger than me. I wasn't long back in Ireland when she went to England."

"You said you worked on the presses in Fleet Street?"

"Yes I did, in the sixties; I spent about ten years in London. Are you in London?"

"Yes I am."

"What part?"

"I live in West Hampstead."

Ted answered, "I know it, at least I did know it, and it's probably all changed now."

"Ted... that song you sang last night, I never heard it before."

"That's not surprising, it never made number one."

"I must say Ted I was surprised to hear places that I know well in London mentioned, Hampstead, Highgate, Chelsea, you knew those places I suppose."

"I did indeed, knew them well, it was many a Saturday afternoon my friends and I spent at Stamford Bridge; often we cheered Chopper Harris on as he tried to cope with the elusive George Best. As Mary Hopkins used to sing, *those were the days*."

"The words of your song, they intrigued me, is it a true story."

Ted took a sip from his drink and said "It is, at least some of it is, it's about the girl, the poet, and about the sixties, all that's true."

"And the famous author part, Is that true?"

"I'm not sure about that."

"Any love or romance attached to it?"

"Oh yes, I suppose you could say without a doubt, it's got a love angle to it."

Paul said, "You are so intrigued with that song, it's all in the past, what difference does it make now?"

"Maybe as a journalist, I have an inquisitive nature, and as a writer it has fired my imagination."

"I'm sure Ted would rather talk about something else."

"No, it's all right Paul; I don't mind talking about it, if I can remember back that far. It's all so long ago, and my memories are all a bit dust covered, sometimes I wonder are they memories, dreams, or my imagination."

"Brush the dust off Ted and let's find out."

"I'll try Jim, but will they reveal the way it was, or the way we thought it was."

"Let's excavate those memories and see what will be revealed."

"Okay Jim you ask the questions, and I'll answer the ones I can."

Chapter Three

"I suppose the first question to ask is, who wrote the poem?"

"I have no idea, I received it in the post, a friend of mine Tony Powell sent it; whether he wrote it or not, I don't know."

"And the poet, the girl in the song, did you know her?"

Ted was silent for a time, staring into his pint then he answered.

"Yes... yes I did, her father owned a second hand book shop and printing business in Belsize Park. Tony Powell often helped out there; it was she who got him the job. As I told you, in the sixties I was working on the printing presses in Fleet Street, and as we all lived around the Swiss Cottage area we often drank in the Swiss Cottage pub with Tony and a great friend of his Ben Mason."

"I know it Ted, that pub is still there, and I often have a drink there."

Ted continued, "As well as the book shop Tony was working part time in Fleet Street on the printing presses. I got to know him, and on our time off we hung around together. You could say he educated himself in that book shop, I know he read fiction, nonfiction, history, biographies, some days when he came in for a pint, he'd pester you with Dickens, the next day it might be Thomas Hardy, Keats, Walter Macken, Wordsworth. One night he came in for a drink, he was all excited about J P Dunleavy's *The Ginger Man*, a fantastic book he said. To say he was well read would be an understatement."

"Do you think the poet in the song became a famous author?"
"I don't know Jim; she must have otherwise why would it be in the poem, but when I left London she was still singing her protest songs and writing her poems."
Paul asked, "What was her name? You haven't told us her name."
Ted took a sip from his pint and said, "Christine... Christine Arkwright."
I asked, "Did she write under that name?"
"She did for her early poems; that's the only name I knew her by; if she became famous, it wasn't under that name; maybe she changed her name in later years."

"But surely if she was on television, or in the papers, you would recognise her."
"I'm not an avid television watcher, if she was on I could have missed her, and if it was under a different name I wouldn't have taken any notice. Since I received that

poem I've visited several bookshops, second hand and new. I've gone to book fairs, I've searched high up and low down, I've flicked the flyleaf of several books and all to no avail.

I've Googled Christine Arkwright, well a friend of mine did, and nothing. Oh he found several Christine Arkwright's but none of them a writer. If Christine got her book published, she didn't give her publisher her real name, or else she has a contract with them not to reveal it. And as I have no idea what name she is now using, or the name of her book, or books. How can I find out if she became an author or not? How can I inquire about an author when I don't know her name?"

Paul asked "do you really think Ted that she would be able to conceal her identity."

"If she took a different name Paul, wrote her book under that name, submitted it to a publisher, told them nothing about her past and said it was her first book. They would have to assume she was who she said she was."

"She just might get away with it" Paul said.

"Ted, the end of the poem" *to a friend for the night we walked over the heath* "was that friend Tony Powell?"

"I don't know Jim, it could be Tony; if it was Christine

who wrote it, but on reading the poem you would assume it was written by a man."

"What was she like?" Paul asked.
Ted paused for a while, and then answered; "beautiful... she was beautiful," his mind conjuring up a picture of her. Then he took a sip from his pint and continued. "The quintessential English rose, blue eyes, straight blonde hair that rested on her shoulders; a fringe cut a fraction above her eyebrows, pale skin, about five foot seven. She could have had any man she wanted, but she was only interested in her writing.
She was a great friend of Tony's, and that's all she remained, though he wanted more. From the very first time he saw her, his life changed, it was as if he had entered a revolving door a care free man, and came out the other side as if he had been struck by lightning."

 Paul said, "You could say he was in love with her then."
"That would be understating it. He loved her from the first moment her saw her, he loved her then; he loves her now and he will love her tomorrow. And when he is dead and in his grave and he has mingled with the dust of the earth; that dust will love her.
They spent a lot of time together, she worked in the bookshop, and she would print her poems and pamphlets there. Tony would go with her on

demonstrations, they would go for a drink together, and as I said they were the best of friends, maybe that's why he left. He wanted more; he pursued her for five or six years and all to no avail. I think he just gave up in the end."

I said, "It must have been hard on him, spending all that time with someone he loved, and her not loving him." "It probably was, but up to the time he left, he always had hoped that she would eventually fall in love with him."
"What was she like Ted? In her ways I mean."
"She was friendly but not pushy; she wouldn't be to the fore in company, she'd engage in conversation with people, but not bombard them. She'd give her opinion and contribute to a debate in her calm quiet way; not loud or over excited, and when she did express an opinion people listened with interest. She had strong opinions on the Vietnam War, and violence in general; you could say she had the mind and opinions of a mature woman more so than a teenager."
I asked Ted, "What kind of poems and songs did she write?"

"I suppose you could say she was a Jodi Mitchell type songwriter, protest songs, some love songs; ballads and some two minute pop tunes, hoping to get some pop group of the day to record them. Poetry...I think she favoured the rhyme and reason type of poem but she also experimented with the avant- garde type which was becoming very popular, what niche she made her mark in, I don't know. Up to the time I left London she hadn't achieved a break through with her songs or poems, but according to the poem she has achieved success as a novelist, and that doesn't surprise me; because she was determined to succeed, and it didn't matter what she had to give up to achieve it."

"So Ted she was a poet, singer, songwriter and musician, and had an interest in world affairs and she only seventeen or eighteen. I must say that's most unusual for a girl so young to know what she wanted from life and to pursue it with such determination. Not for, her teenage parties, teenage love, dating; dancing, fashion and drooling over some pop star, none of the things that occupy young minds."

"Oh she was well up to date with her fashion Jim; all the latest dresses, skirts, tops, blouses; she very rarely wore jeans or trousers suits, her dresses and skirts always at a discreet length, not for her the all revealing micro minie of the day. And she was well aware of all the pop songs and singers."

"She fascinates me Ted, just talking about her makes me wish I had known her, I hope she fulfilled her dreams, and if she did at what expense? Anyway whoever wrote the poem, whether it was Tony, Christine, or someone else they know the name she writes under now, but where is Tony Powell? And where is Christine Arkwright?"

"I don't know, I have no idea, maybe he eventually returned to London, but one thing I do know, whatever part of the world he's in, he's still in love with Christine and always will be."

"Why did he leave London?"

"I don't know Jim maybe it was because of Christine, as I said he was in love with her, but as far as she was concerned it was just friendship. I never remember her being with anyone."

Paul said, "Maybe... she was gay or whatever, back then she would have to hide it, gay people were treated as undesirables and second class citizens."

"They are some present day dinosaurs Paul that still look upon them that way. I don't know if she was gay or not, and I don't care, I never saw her with a man or woman. You must remember she was only seventeen or eighteen when they met, all she was interested in at that time was her writing, and everything else played second fiddle."

"Maybe as she got older and her career took off, she found someone" I said.

"I think that was one of the reasons why Tony left. I think it eventually dawned on him that no matter how much he loved her, that she would never love him. That he was on a road to nowhere, that friends is all they ever would be and the thought of her being with someone else... maybe someday meet them walking down the street, hand in hand. He just could not accept that, he couldn't cope with that, so he left,
Out of sight, out of mind."

"I would say out of sight Jim, but never out of mind."

"Did he leave before you or after you?"

"Before me, he just packed up and went, one day he was there, and then he was gone. A few weeks later I got a Letter from him from Australia, we were into the seventies then, and some of the old gang had moved on or married.

I wanted a change, so I to went to Australia and from there to America. I worked and travelled around there for a few years, went in search of Donna and found her, heard she was married, moved on without seeing her. I decided to come back here for a year or two, and I'm still here, I guess I'm here to stay now."

"Did you and Tony ever meet in Australia?"

"No Jim, we never met."

"Who's Donna?" Paul asked.

"Maybe someday I'll tell you."

"London in the sixties Ted, it must have been exiting."

"It sure was Jim, *the swinging sixties* they call it, and Tony and I certainly swung with it. We were both from a rural area, and city life was some change for us. Can you imagine? One day standing in a field somewhere in Ireland, and the next day in the middle of London. But we soon got the hang of it. The Beetles, the Stones, Minie skirts, flower power free love, I tell you Jim, it was something to sit outside the Swiss Cottage on a summers evening and watch all the young girls walk by."

"Did ye avail of it Ted?"

"Avail of what Paul?"

"Avail of all that free love!"

"What do you think? We were young and ready for anything, the world was ours, and the consequences didn't matter. We all hung around together, we'd all meet in the Swiss Cottage, have a pint or two and get a taxi to Hampstead, have a pint in the Railway bar."

I said, "It's still there Ted, it's called the garden now."

"And then we'd walk over the heath to Highgate, and on the way back have a swim in one of the ponds. As a matter of fact it was because of a swim in one of those ponds I met Donna."

"Maybe Tony could help us" I said.

"I have no doubt he could, but he's not here, and I have no idea where he is. All I have is the words of that song; do you think that is enough for a story?"

"I don't know Ted; the poem is mostly about the girl, maybe if we knew a bit more about what the guys were up too. Would you write out the words of it for me; I'd like to study it."

"Sure... but I have an idea Jim, you say you want a story, well maybe you can have your story. You can use your imagination, maybe you can use the words of the song to produce a work of fiction or maybe half truth and half fiction, you tell the story as if you are Tony Powell, the words of the song and what I have told you should help. You know Tony met her when she was a teenager, you know she was a poet, you know Tony fell in love with her, she didn't love him, you know he left London. You can assume that she became a famous author, maybe they have got together again, maybe not, and you can tell the story of Tony Powell and Christine Arkwright."

"I don't think so Ted, it would be better to know the truth, to have Tony Powell tell it himself. If I do what you say, it would be just another work of fiction. It would be nice to get a story without resorting to fiction. I don't mean an all action car chasing, bang, bang; he shot me down kind of story, but an everyday story of ordinary people. A story of dreams fulfilled, or unfilled, of happiness or sadness. A story of love, requited or unrequited, a story about the way ninety per cent of people live their life."

"I don't think you could compare Tony, or Christine to ninety per cent of the people Jim."

"Maybe not, but if there is a story, we'll never know unless we can contact one of them."

"But do you think there is a need to contact them; surely the poem can be the basis for your story, and what I've told you."

"It would be nice to know what became of them Ted."

"You know what became of them, Tony went to Australia and according to the poem Christine became a writer."

"It would be nice to know what happened after that Ted, for instance did they meet again".

"Does it matter? You'll surely get a story from the sixties; up to the time he went to Australia as a matter of fact that could be a good ending to your book."

"I don't know Ted, look let's wait and see if it's worth pursuing as a story before we worry about the ending of it. I'll be back in London next week, I'll make some inquiries maybe someone somewhere know of them."

Chapter Four

I had enjoyed my stay in Ireland. And back in London as some other members of our staff were on holidays I was extremely busy at the paper. I had to put Christine Arkwright, Tony Powell and Ted Patterson to the back of my mind. It was at least a month before I got a chance to make any enquiries. And then one evening I walked to Swiss Cottage. I stood there taking in the scene, to my right the red brick cinema, on my left, Swiss Cottage Library, and in the fork of Finchley Road and Avenue Road, stood the Swiss Cottage Pub.

I thought, it's over forty years since Tony Powell and his contemporaries stood here looking at this scene, where are they all now? I knew Ted Patterson was in Ireland, where was Christine Arkwright? Was she still alive? What name did she write under? Where was Tony Powell? I walked down to the library and entered. I walked up the steps and stood in the display area looking around. I decided to go to the lending library; I approached the desk and said to the Librarian,

"Excuse me could you tell me if you have you any books in stock by an author named Christine Arkwright?"

The Librarian consulted her computer and said, "I'm sorry we have no author by that name."

I said, "Poetry, fiction, nonfiction, anything at all?"

Again she said, "Sorry, nothing is showing under that name."

I asked her, "How I would find an author if I didn't know her name, or the name of any book she wrote."

She answered; "I think it would be quite impossible, you would need some reference to the name she, or he writes under, or a name of one of their books."

"The name I've just mentioned, how I would find the name she is now writing under."

"You can't, not unless she wants you to, if under her present writing name she has made no reference to her birth name in her books or on her web site, and if she has an agreement with her publishers not to reveal that name; then I'm afraid your task is impossible. If she had made reference to her birth name, then when I typed in that name it would tell me the name she is using now. It's quite possible we have her books on our shelves; you could pick one up and browse through it, but you would have no idea it was written by the person whose name you gave me."

"Thanks for your help."

"You're welcome."

Leaving the library I realised that it was going to be impossible to find out what name Christine is writing under. I decided to go for a pint in the Swiss Cottage. The barman was a young Asian, no point in asking him about Tony Powell. I called for a pint of strong ale, paid him, went outside and sat down to observe the scene. Cars, buses, taxies, trucks, people from all walks of life and from various countries, and all different creeds and races passed up and down before me. It reminded me of a disoriented ant hill.

The people who sat here around forty years ago viewed a similar scene, apart from a change in the vehicles and fashion, well maybe not so much the fashion, but definitely the vehicles. I tried to imagine what must have been going through Tony Powell's and Ted Patterson's mind when for the first time as eighteen year olds from rural Ireland they sat here observing this scene, I thought what a change for them, to be living in isolation one day in the country, and the next day here in the middle of London.

 I finished my drink, brought the empty glass to the counter, said thanks to the barman and walked out to the sunlit street. I decided to walk to Belsize Park, to see if the book shop was still there. As I had no idea where in Belsize Park it might be, I decided to ask an elderly couple who were walking towards me.

I said, "Excuse me I'm looking for a second hand book shop, I was told it's in this area."

The man answered, "It was, it closed many years ago. It's a Laundromat now."

"Do the same people own it?"

The woman answered, "No they sold and moved on ages ago."

"Do you know where to?"

"No, they closed the shop, put up a, *for sale sign*, and they were gone within a month."

"Did you know them?" The man asked.

"No but a friend of mine knew them and their daughter."

"We didn't know the daughter that well, I think she moved away from here when she finished college, became a journalist or a writer or something like that."

"Did she change her name when she became a writer?"

"We don't know, we never heard of her since she left, she could be writing under a different name, maybe that's why we haven't heard of her."

I thanked them for the information.

"Hope we were of some help to you."

I asked, "Do you think would the owners of the Laundromat, know where they moved to."

The woman answered, "I doubt it, they opened that

business only about six months ago, the book shop must be closed well over thirty years now, the Laundromat is only one of several businesses that's come and gone through the years."

I said, "Goodbye and thanks again."

"Good luck with your search."

Back in my flat I made a cup of coffee then checked my email. One from Paul...

I met Ted Paterson in the pub last night. He said he has received an envelope from Tony Powell, a kind of diary, he wants to meet you. Can you come over?

I phoned Paul and said, "I don't know if I should come over, I've been making some enquiries about Christine and I think we're wasting our time, it's going to be impossible to find her."

"We might find something in the diaries that might help," Paul said.

"That's a possibility. I'll talk to my editor he might give me a week in Ireland to pursue it; we might get something out of it that we can use in the paper."

"Right Jim; give me a buzz if you are coming over."

I explained the situation to my editor. He thought it might be worth having a look at the diaries.

"Take a week", he said, "And maybe you might come up with something that might be of interest to our readers."

I phoned Paul and told him I was coming over on Friday and could he meet me at the airport.

Chapter Five

It was a lovely summer's evening; I was looking out the window of the plane at the wonderful scenery as we flew over Dunmore, then Tramore, and landed at Waterford Airport. My mind had been occupied on the flight, wondering what was in the envelope that Tony Powell had sent. I thought it a bit of a coincidence, that just as I was trying to track down Tony Powell, Ted got an envelope containing some kind of diary from him. But coincidence or not, I was looking forward to reading it.

As Waterford is a small rural airport it didn't take me long to retrieve my luggage, and within twenty minutes of landing I was sitting in Paul's car, a two thousand and twelve Mazda six; and according to Paul any other make of car in the world just couldn't compete with it.
I said, "I'll have to find someplace to stay for the week, can you recommend some place?"
"I sure can our house."
"No I couldn't impose on you."
"Nonsense, Mother insists so no more about it."

Within three quarters of an hour of leaving the airport we were stopped outside Paul's house, which was two miles outside the Village, a mile from the coast and about eleven miles from Waterford City. Paul's mother, Helen came out to meet me and inquired about my mother and father and asked "when did you visit them last?"

I answered, "last Sunday, I had dinner with them."

"How are they?"

"Great and they send their regards."

"You're just in time for dinner, lovely fresh mackerel; Paul went to Boatstrand for them, and new potatoes, *British Queens*, fresh from the garden."

After dinner Paul and I walked to the sea, Paul said "Ted Patterson will be in the pub at about half nine."

"Will he bring the diary?"

"I don't know, he didn't say."

I told Paul about the inquiries I had made about Tony Powell and Christine Arkwright in London, all to no avail. He said, "If there is a story worth telling maybe the diaries will throw some light on it."

"I hope so, because I don't think pursuing Christine Arkwright will be any help to us."

At half nine Paul and I were sitting in a corner of the pub, enjoying a pint.

"There's a good few in tonight."

"Holiday time Jim, we might even get a bit of a sing song later."

At about ten o' clock Ted Patterson walked in.

Paul called him over to join us.

I asked "What are you having?"

"I'll have a bottle of Guinness."

I got the drink.

Ted said "Cheers, I needed that."

"Tony sent you a diary?"

"Yes, a letter and I suppose a bit more than a diary, quite a few small note books, and a kind of a record of some of the things they were up too in the sixties. He thinks that the contents of the note books could have the makings of a story. He is hoping that I might know someone who would be interested in writing it; where ever he got that idea from I don't know."

"Did you read them?" Paul asked.

"I read the short letter he sent with them and I scouted through the diaries, nothing in them about the present, as far as I can ascertain from the quick look I had, they start around nineteen sixty four and finish at the start of the seventies."

"Any mention of the name Christine might be writing under? Did the letter have his address on it?"

"No Jim, no address on the letter, and remember the diaries were written before she became an author, so I don't think we're going to find her pen name in them. Plenty about Christine though, Donna also gets a mention; it looks like all shall be revealed."

"So we are as wise as ever" Paul said.

"I wouldn't say that, I'm sure they will be of better value to Jim for a story than the poem, when we read through them they will surely tell us something."

"Did you bring them with you?"

"No Jim, I thought it might be better if you called around to my place tomorrow, I didn't want the customers gawking at us, I brought the poem, or the song, call it what you like. You said Jim that you wished you had known Christine; maybe you can get to know her through these diaries."

"Yes... yes it would have been great to have known a woman such as her, poet, musician, singer and songwriter. I suppose the only hope I have of getting to know her now in some form is through the diaries, you said you have the poem, would you read it? I'd love to hear all of it."

Paul said "Wait until I get another round, and called to the barmaid, two pints and a bottle of Guinness please."

Ted said, "Okay Jim here we go."

Over The Heath

*She was a poet in her teens, her pen just wrote down the
truth,*
*but the truth is often ignored, they called her a pot
smoking youth.*
*They put her down as a beatnik; well she did wear a
flower in her hair,*
*maybe she was a bit off beat, but in her heart she really
did care.*
*Her compositions she sent to the papers, she
complained about apartheid and hate,*
*she was against the war in Vietnam, and they called her
a red in the States.*
*When trouble broke out in Ulster she said, they must
have equal rights,*
*if those at the top won't listen, thousand's will die in the
fight.*

Paul said, "There are no doubt that's definitely the
sixties, beatniks, flowers in her hair and all that." Ted
continued.

*I remember the first day I met her, she said peace, not
war, is the way,*
*We were sitting on a bar stool in Chelsea, debating who
shot J F K.*

She joined in ban the bomb marches, her protest songs she loudly would sing,
Dismayed she wept on my shoulder, when she heard they had shot Luther King.
Some mornings she'd watch from her window as the postman came to her door,
feeling a bit down she would listen, as the rejection slips fell on the floor.
I met her one day in Hampstead; she was busking with friends on the street,
we went to a cafe for coffee, and then we walked over the heath.

"J F K, Martin Luther King, ban the bomb marches, that's also the sixties" I said.

We sat on a park bench in Highgate, and talked all through the night,
at the break of the dawn I convinced her that she should continue to write.
Next day I was leaving for Ireland, she kissed me good bye on the train,
many years have gone by since we parted now and then she drifts through my brain.
I had, no doubt she was gifted, that she would find fortune and fame,
one day when I opened the paper, and in the book page

I saw her name.
The critics couldn't find words to praise her, they said,
it's the book of the year,
I was so glad she had made it; there and then I gave out
a loud cheer.

I said, "That verse starts in the sixties, but where does it finish? It says *many years have gone by since we parted,* how many? How long did it take her to get published? Was it in the seventies, eighties, nineties? Or was it in this Century? And the poem was written after she became famous, because whoever wrote it knew she had changed her name, otherwise they wouldn't have recognised it in the paper. Go on Ted finish it."

Many years it took them to listen, to the words that she
had to say,
many years of hatred and killing, and they are still killing
today.
All young people out there I beg you, ignore the bomb
and the gun,
whoever gets killed, remember they are some Mother's
daughter or son.
Now in the twenty first century, you youth of the World
have your say,
you must try and persuade all our leaders, that peace,
not war, is the way.

As I went to the book shop that evening, I thought, she
now has the World at her feet,
and as I flicked the fly leaf I read, to a friend for the
night we walked over the heath.

Paul said, "The end of the last verse is the here and
now, which tells us the poem is relatively new."
I said, "I agree, but who wrote it? Was it Christine?
Tony? Or someone who knew them, again at the
beginning of the last verse, it refers to *many years*. Any
idea Ted, from the time she kissed him goodbye on the
train to seeing her name in the paper, how many
years?"
"I have no idea Jim, it could be last year, it could be
thirty years ago; if he did see her name in the paper?
Did Tony write it? Did Christine write it? Maybe it's
fiction, just a figment of some ones imagination.
If it was Tony, maybe it's his way of saying, she hasn't
forgotten me there's hope for me yet. If it was Christine
maybe she's reminiscing about the past."
I said, "If it is fiction we are looking for the name of an
author that doesn't exist, and the name of a book which
may never have been written."

"Maybe the diaries will throw some light on it," Paul
said.
Ted answered, "I doubt it, as I said they are mostly

about the sixties, they end at the start of the seventies, and I'm sure Christine hadn't changed her name at that time."

"Everything about this fascinates me Ted, Christine, the diaries, the poem, by the end of the week I hope I have something for my editor."

Ted said, "Then come around to my place tomorrow, and we'll have a look at the diaries to see what they will reveal, in the mean time let's have a few more pints and enjoy the songs."

Chapter Six

At ten thirty on Saturday morning, I was walking towards Ted's cottage, which was about a mile from the village and about a mile from Paul's house. Ted had bought it when he returned to Ireland and had extended on to it, a bathroom, bedroom and a small sun lounge. It was neat and tidy, and Ted didn't get carried away during the Celtic tiger years and built a J R Ewing, "South Fork" size house. He was sitting in the sun lounge drinking a mug of coffee when I arrived.

"Come in and sit yourself down."
I said, "You have a lovely place here Ted, warm and cosy, and a real sun trap."
"That's the idea, the sun shines into this room most of the day, I can sit here without a fire and save on fuel, I'll get you a coffee, or do you want something stronger?"
"No thanks, not at this time of day, I had too much last night, a coffee will do."
Ted went and made the coffee, came back with it and said, "Tony sent a short typed letter with the diaries, we'll call them that for the want of a better name, he said when he returned to Ireland he had intended to write about our time in London.

He was very enthusiastic at first. He was writing mostly from memory, so he only wrote of some events, I guess those events stood out in his mind more than others. He asks if I remember some things, to add them to what he has written and maybe I might get some kind of story from them.

In his letter he explains how he intended to write, no dates or year, but he goes into quite some details about some events and they have quite a few pages. These have been at the bottom of a drawer for a long time now; he said he found them while having a clear out. He thought maybe I'd be interested in them, so anyway this is what we have."

Ted started to read Tony's letter.

This is not intended to be a record of everyday events as they happened, but it will be an occasional account of the way things were. I intend to detail some of the events that happened back then, some great times with good friends. I will record them as they come to mind and not in any special order, I may write of something that happened around nineteen seventy and then I might revert to the early sixties.

As we go through our life, some parts of that life are of more interest to us than others, I've decided to record in writing a part of my life that I found most interesting, and that was London in the sixties, starting around nineteen sixty three when men and women became liberated. This may be of interest to only myself, if that is the case, so be it, but as I have nothing much else to do it helps to pass the time.

As I am writing from memory, I will not give dates or year, sometimes I will record the events as they come to mind, a day or two, or maybe a weekend, and then my next entry could be a week, a month or a year later or earlier. I hope to write this, not as someone looking back on past events, but as if those events are happening now. I will only write of events that took place in the sixties because in the seventies most of us had gone our separate ways and what happened after that is of no consequence. I hope that between the poem and these note books that you or someone you know maybe able concoct some kind of story. If you think these events are not story materials and are of no interest to you; then feel free to dispose of them anyway you see fit.

Sing me a song of the sixties and help me to turn back the clock,
to when life was easy and swinging and we were starting to rock.
The world was young and never ending, we had youth on our side,

and on the radio great music, that caused a sensation worldwide.

I hope this little verse will jog your memory.

Regards

Tony.

"Tony seems to be of the same opinion as you Ted, any story should be confined to the sixties; and even includes a short verse to remind you of the sixties; you said you haven't read the diaries."
"That's right Jim, just a quick look, they tell of our time in London in the sixties, most of them are about Tony, Christine and a few more friends; here have a look."

They were written with pen, some bits crossed out and some additions here and there.
I said, "Do you think you can add something to them Ted?"
"I don't know, it's over forty years ago; maybe reading them now, and with you and Paul asking questions, it might clear some of the dust from my memories."
Paul arrived with some fresh mackerel for Ted.
"Were you fishing?" Ted asked.
"No, I drove to Boatstrand for them, they're very fresh; mother cleaned them, any luck with the diaries?"

I answered, "Not yet, just Tony explaining how he intended to write."

"You take them with you Jim."

"No Ted I'd rather read them here with you, if I need clarification on some things, you can explain them to me, do you mind if Paul and I call around six thirty this evening, we can go through them, and go for a few pints afterwards."

"No bother, I'll have my dinner finished by then, these mackerel and a few new spuds, and then a few pints, what more could a man ask for, I'll see you later."

Paul and I passed the afternoon swimming at the cove, and at five o'clock were sitting in Helen's dining room eating dinner. At six we were on our way to Ted's. Helen had offered to drive us, but we declined the offer, saying we needed the walk after such a big dinner.

Helen asked, "What time will you be home?"

Paul answered, "We'll be at Ted's until around nine thirty, and then the three of us are walking to the Village for a drink. It's a good fine night we might walk home, and we'll see you later."

Ted made three mugs of tea when we arrived, and sitting in his house, the evening sun casting long shadows across the lawn, he handed me a note book, saying, "Now let's see what Tony wrote about."

I said, "If I read them, both of you will be sitting there twiddling your thumbs."

Paul said, "I think you should read it to us Ted."

"What! Me?"

I agreed with Paul, saying, "You were there, you will probably recognise some of the events that are in them, and we can ask questions if we want to."

Ted reluctantly agreed and said okay, "Here we go."

I took a note book and pen from my pocket and said to Ted, "Would you mind if I take some notes".

"It makes no difference to me, now can I introduce you to Tony Powell's diaries, and the sixties?"

Chapter Seven

It was around five o'clock on a sunny evening in June, Ted Patterson, and I, my name is Tony Powell were sitting outside the *Swiss Cottage Pub* in Swiss Cottage, drinking a pint of ale with our friend Ben Mason, a true Cockney, born within the sound off Bow Bells. He was about six three in height and built to match and had the reputation of someone you didn't mess with. We were admiring the scenery which consisted of cars, buses, taxis and of course plenty of girls, the younger ones wearing Mini Skirts.

The pub stood in the busy junction of Finchley Rd and Avenue Rd. Across from us was the Odeon cinema and on our right, the entrance to Swiss Cottage tube station and at the other side of the pub was Swiss Cottage library, which the Queen had officially opened in nineteen sixty four, and where Ben worked as a Library attendant, starting at eight in the morning and finishing at two one week, and the next week starting at two and finishing at nine, this enabled him to do some part time work as a bouncer or doorman.
Ted worked full time on the printing presses in Fleet Street, and sometimes when they were short staffed

either through holidays or sick leave, he got me an odd shift there

Ben asked me, "Are you enjoying the view? Or would you rather be at home?"
I said, "If I was at home now I'd probably be standing on top of a hill looking at some cows grazing in the valley below, now if I could transfer these minie clad beauties to that valley, maybe then I'd rather be at home, but as I can't do that, I think right now, I'm quite happy to be here."
Ben said, "Cor blimey mate, look at that," as a long legged damsel walked by, then said, "the weekend lies ahead, tell me Tony what have ye planned? And what direction will you come to work from on Monday?"
"What do you mean?" I asked.

"Some of the lads were saying in the pub during the week that you have come to work from several different directions on a couple of Monday mornings".
"All I can say, it's not my fault if some of those lovely young things you see passing by here feel sorry for me and want to take me home and Mother me for the weekend, who am I to say no."
Ted went to the bar for another three pints.

Ben said, "Now fellows I think when we have these drinks finished we should go to Hampstead, for a walk on the heath. Get some grass under your feet, and think of home, and as it's so warm and sultry, have a dip in one of the ponds, then have a few pints in the railway bar, and finish up back here."

I answered, "Sounds good to me, but we haven't any swimming togs."

Ben answered, "It should be quiet by the time we get there; we won't need them."

^

I interrupted Ted, saying, "If he continues to write like that we'll soon have all the information we require."

"True Jim, but remember these were written before Christine changed her name, so he can't reveal it to us."

"Maybe back in the sixties when writing her poetry and lyrics she might have used a pen name, Tony might mention it."

"Maybe Jim; but the only name I ever heard Tony call her was Christine."

Paul asked, "What does he mean? When he says, *coming to work from different directions.*"

Ted answered "You must remember Paul this was London in the sixties the contraceptive pill had brought great changes, it was a time of anything goes, people shook off their conservative attitudes and became more liberated.

Young women and men moved out from home and got their own bedsits and flats, or as some referred to them, their own pads. And when they went out dancing and drinking at weekends, they were no boundaries, they usually ended up sleeping together.

Everyone went a little mad; it was like the boom years here with the banks and borrowing, no sense of responsibility, and no one thinking of the consequences. We were young, carefree and reckless, and tomorrow or the day after didn't exist. So if Tony, Ben or I met a girl in a bar or club on a Friday or Saturday night, we would go back to their place and go to work from there on Monday morning."

"And all this sex for free."

"Nothing is for free, we all pay Paul, one way or another, some picked up sexual transmitted diseases, and some paid with their freedom."

I said, "Paid with their freedom?"

"That's right Jim, when you used a condom you could see it, you knew it was there, the pill changed everything, it was invisible, had they taken it or not? No nothing is free Jim.

Some men seek out a prostitute, that's a blue chip investment, *pay the woman or leave the bed*. And then you have the speculators with more money than sense, expensive gifts, top class restaurants, wine and dine, take a chance and hope it pays off. One way or the other we are all going to pay, and what are we paying for? We are paying for man's natural instinct to enter paradise, that fathomless zone off perpetual pleasure."

I said, "you are cynical Ted, what about the man and woman who fall in love and live happily ever after? What about men like Tony Powell, you said he was in love then, and he is still in love today."
"Ted answered, "You will always have exceptions, I'm talking majority Jim. Some soldiers join the army for the love of their country, and then they are the mercenary soldiers, the ones who sell to the highest bidder, in all walks of life, you will find the mercenaries."
Paul said, "Read some more Ted."
Ted said, "Now where were we... Ah yes, skinny dipping, and continued with the diaries."

We finished our drinks and walked up through Belsize Park to Hampstead High Street, down past Keats house and on to the heath. A lot of people were availing of the fine evening to go walking, but as we travelled further on to the heath it got quieter. A few fishermen were scattered around the lake banks, but far enough away from us not to notice whether we had a togs on or not, the evening was humid and warm.

Ben said, "See that pontoon in the middle of the pond, we'll swim from this pontoon out to that one, have a rest and then back to this one."

We all dived in, butt naked and swam towards the pontoon, Ted who was not used to clear water swimming, began to struggle and had to veer towards the nearest bank, when he was near the bank he went to stand up and found himself waist deep in mud. As he struggled to haul himself clear, a female voice said, "Let me give you a hand."

∧

I said, "Surely Ted, you remember that?"

"How could I ever forget, I nearly drowned that evening. It was my first time swimming in fresh water; the pontoon was further out than I thought, I had to divert towards the bank, I only barely made it. I was relieved as I knelt there waist deep in mud, and then I heard a woman's voice offering to help me out, and me with no togs on. Would you believe she was an American and staying in a nearby hotel?"

"What happened then Ted?" Paul asked

"I told Tony what happened, so I'll let him tell you," and Ted continued to read.

"She asked "Can you reach my hand."

"No worries, I'm okay; I'll manage myself."

"I don't think so; you seem to be well and truly stuck."
I pointed to the pontoon and said, "My friends and I were swimming."
"Why are you in here then instead of out there with them?"
"It was too far, I had to divert, I didn't realise there were so much mud."
"You seem to be enjoying it she said, you won't let me help you out."
"To tell the truth, we, I have no togs on."

"You were skinny dipping? I do the same back home, in a lake in the middle of our Ranch, not in the centre of a City. Here give me your hand, with all that mud I won't see anything, and when you're out you can wrap my jacket around you, and we'll go get your clothes."
I caught her hand, and she hauled me out. I wrapped her jacket around me, and we walked around for my clothes.
"Your jacket is ruined I said."
She answered; "Never mind, if you put on your clothes they will also be ruined. You wait here, I'll go get my car, and we'll drive back to the hotel and you can have a shower."

^

Ted turned the page of the diary, "That's it he said, I guess he didn't get around to finishing it."
Paul said, "Come on Ted don't keep us in suspense surely you must remember what happened next."

"I remember it well, I'll tell you no lie Paul; she came back in her car, a Mini Cooper, we drove to her Hotel, she told me she was from Texas, and she was a beautiful woman, tall, blonde, about twenty years of age. I told her I had often heard of the *Yellow Rose of Texas* but I never thought I'd meet her. When we got to the Hotel I showered, got dressed and I thanked her for all her help."
And that's all"? Paul said.

"No not quite, what could have been a disastrous evening turned out well in the end. I told her I was going down to the Railway bar to meet my fellow skinny dippers, she offered to drive me, and I said it's only around the corner, we can walk. And so we did, we had several drinks, then back to the Hotel, and I didn't leave until seven o' clock Monday morning.
She stayed in London for about six weeks, we met on several occasions, we drove down to Hastings, and we had a wonderful time.
It was 1966, and they were big celebrations for William the Conqueror's defeat of King Harold at the battle of

Hastings in 1066; pageantry, re-enactments and all that. During the day Medieval Knights and at night a storm of electrified passion, and after the storm, a period of calm and quietness, and as you lay there contemplating on it all, the urge to begin again. We both understood what it was, a fling, a wonderful six week fling, and then we went our separate ways. I never met her again, she send me a Christmas card once, but not anymore.

I said, "And if you believe that Paul, you will believe anything."
"It's true Jim, Paul asked me about Donna remember, I told him I'd tell him about her some day and now I have, I can prove it, give me a minute."
Ted went and searched a drawer of a desk in the corner of the room, then said, "Here it is," and handed me a Christmas card.
I read. *Hi Muddy, hope you're still young enough to go skinny dipping, happy Christmas, Donna.*
"Who's Muddy?" Paul asked.
Ted answered, "I am, that's what Donna always called me."
I said, "I'm sorry if I doubted you Ted, it all seemed so farfetched."
"In these diaries some of the things we got up to will seem very farfetched and unrealistic, but they happened. As a matter of fact reminiscing about Donna

brought another event to my mind, but right now I think we should repair to the pub for a few pints."

Chapter Eight

As we walked the road to the Village I commented on the wild flowers and the scent they gave off, meadowsweet, willow herb, foxglove, wild woodbine, and loosestrife, just to name a few. Walking the streets of London all you can smell is the fumes, "No wonder you want to stay here." I said.

Paul answered, "It's lovely now, but you should be here in winter, the wind roaring in from the sea, playing a lament on the electric wires, rain, fog, drizzle. A reprieve from that when the wind swings around to the north east, blowing so sharp if you put your head out the window it would shave you, one bad and the other worse."

"Swings and roundabouts," I said.

The pub was almost full. The local team had played a football match and had won and were now celebrating, and loud in praise of each other's exploits on the field of play.

Ted said, "We'll move into the other bar it's quieter there."

I called for three pints of Guinness.

Ted said, "No thanks Jim, you and Paul have your pints;

I'll get a bottle of Guinness and a small glass, it will last me longer, I can't drink like I used to."

"Are you sure?"

"I'm certain."

Paul asked Ted, "What else came to your mind when you were reminiscing about Donna?"

"A man called Paddy O Conner."

"Who was he?" I asked.

"He was an Irishman who made history."

"In what way did he make history?" Paul asked.

"He was employed as a bus inspector."

I asked, "What's historical about that."

"Not that, the fact is he was the first Irish Mayor of the London Borough of Camden."

"And what was your connection to him?"

"I had no connection with him, but Tony and Ben went to his inauguration party."

"Did they know him?"

"No Jim, but he held his party in the gymnasium and swimming pool complex across from the Library where Ben worked, and he had a bet with the security there that he and Tony would attend the party."

"And did they?" Paul asked.

"They sure did."

"Tell us." I said.

"I think we should wait to see if it is in the diary, I'm sure Tony would have had all the details."

The players celebrating their victory started a sing song, and after a few songs they asked Ted to sing. He was reluctant at first, but they insisted, and he relented in the end.
"What are you going to sing?" I asked.
"I'll try this one; it's called *Permanent Tear.*"

In the morning when waking my heart is aching, I realise I'm all alone / there's just me only, I am so lonely ever since you left our home.
My heart is broken, so I go to my local, I'm drinking whiskey and beer / my friends they come by, and each of them tries to dry up this permanent tear.
The band it is playing, the dancers are swaying but I don't hear them at all / because you're not here and without my dear I can never walk tall.
I pick up my phone, I call her home, her Mother says she's not here / she has left you, she's found someone new, once more that permanent tear

Chorus

I've got the blues the permanent blues ever since you said good bye / I've got the blues the permanent blues and a permanent tear in my eye / to me you were so

*good, without you I'm no good why did you go away /
now that you're gone, I can't go on, I can't get through
the day.*

*I go to my bed, I lay down my head, but I can't get any
sleep / I stare at the ceiling, such a sad feeling once
more I'm starting to weep.*
*The nights are much colder, and I long to hold her, and
oh how I wish she was here / and God knows I miss her
and I long to kiss her and dry up this permanent tear.*
*Outside it is raining; inside I'm paining as I wonder
where it went wrong / my mind says let go, my heart is
saying no, it won't accept she has gone.*
*It just won't believe it that she would deceive it and
throw away all of those years / but it's no use
pretending, there's no happy ending; I must live with
this permanent tear.*

The song got a great reception from the footballers.
"I never heard that before." Paul said.
Ted Answered, "It was Christine who wrote it, she used
to sing it sometimes when busking."
Paul said "if she didn't make it as a writer; she could
definitely have made it as a singer- songwriter, that's a
good song."
"Did she write many songs?" I asked Ted.
"I think so, she used to sing them at rallies and when

59

she went busking. I don't think she ever recorded any, not back then anyway, her big interest was prose and poetry."

"I don't think we can find Christine Ted, we have no reference to her name as a writer, and do you think we have any hope of finding Tony Powell."

"Only if he wants us to find him Jim, as for Christine, maybe as we go through the diaries we might find something, a clue, something. If there is something to find, maybe she never became an author, or famous, maybe she continued working in the book shop until it was sold and then moved with her parents to where ever they moved to, and got a job in an office or something. But do we need to find them, does it matter what became of them? Can't you just write about what's in the diaries, what happened afterwards have no bearing on the diaries."

I answered, "It would be nice to know what became of them."

Paul said, "Maybe Tony is just romanticising everything, his mind conjuring up the way he wanted it to be, not the way it really was, a one way love that existed forty years ago, and apart from him everyone else has long forgotten. Is the poem true or not? If she didn't become a famous author, will we still continue, or do we pack it in right now?"

I answered; "I think we should continue, even if Christine never became an author, I think we can still get a story from their exploits in the sixties, and I do think the poem is true, and my editor has allowed me a week. I must be back at my desk Monday week with something for the paper."

After breakfast on Sunday morning, Paul and his mother went to mass, I walked to the cove, when I got there I saw Ted sitting on a rock looking out to sea.
"How is the head?" I asked.
"Grand; I thought you'd be at mass."
"I gave it a skip and you?"
"I haven't been for years."
"Don you believe?"
"I'm not sure Jim, it's just, I mean, I seem to believe in something different than they do. It's all so organised, collective thinking; they are all like Robots, as if they had no mind of their own. It's all just a repeat, the same mantra every day."
"That's what organised religion is Ted."

"I know Jim, the trouble is I was never organised in my life, I never cared for any kind of organisation, I think all organisations are only looking after their own interest. Is it possible to believe in Jesus? Be a Christian, and not believe in the church."

"I think so Ted; the church as we know it today didn't exist in the time of Jesus and it is as far removed from his teachings that the moon is from the earth. Jesus had nothing to do with Cannon law, so I suppose you can have Jesus without the church. Obey his laws, and not be concerned about those laws added by the church. But some people need the church, they can't cope unless someone is telling them what to do Ted, they need organising, they need organisations, they need order in their lives, as individuals they can't cope. And then you have the people like you Ted, people who are suspicious of authority, who must question everything, people who must analyse everything, turn it inside out to see what makes it tick."

"Is that how you see me Jim, maybe I am like that, maybe I'm not. But give me the choice to sit here, looking at the sea, the cliffs, the horizon, the clouds, the waves, the birds; or sit in a crowded church repeating the same mantra as everybody else, and gazing at manmade icons, then you will find me here.
If there is a God, and he made all this, then why shouldn't I sit here and admire and appreciate his work, and as you say, analyse it all, question it, turn it inside out. But no matter how I analyse it or question it, I still can't understand it, where did it all come from. Did it come from God?

Is it evolution? Where is it all going? Where are we going? And yet, I don't know whether I believe or not, sometimes I ask myself why can't I believe when minds far superior to mine believe. Sometimes I can accept without doubt that it is evolution, and yet again in some way I can see God in it all. Does that make sense?"

"I guess, it's hard to fathom it all Ted; our minds cannot comprehend the vastness of space, the never ending distance; surely a logical mind would say, on the law of averages other forms of life must exist, and if they do exist; is our God their God? Did he create them as well as us, and that brings us full circle; God or evolution? All we can do is our best, and hope when the end comes, we got it right."

Dark clouds gathered on the horizon, the summer breeze of the morning turned to a strong wind, the sea was beginning to churn up a bit.
Ted said, "I think it's going to get a bit damp."
"I think it's going to be a wetness more than damp Ted, the forecast is for a very wet afternoon, it will make a good evening to go through the diaries."
"Come on, let's walk home it's getting a bit chilly here, we can have a coffee at my place."
"No thanks Ted not for me, the dinner will be ready; I don't want to be late."

"Okay Jim, call around when it suits you, bring Paul with you, and we'll see what the diaries will reveal."

The afternoon was wet and windy, so Helen drove us to Ted's, and said, "I'll pick you up at tea time."
"How was mass?" Ted asked Paul.
"The usual" Paul answered.
"Ted and I spent the morning observing creation, Ted has a foot in both camps, he can't decide between God and evolution."
Ted answered; "A visionary mind can see beyond the horizon," and asked, "Would you like tea or coffee?"
We both said tea.
Paul said, "Ted... about Donna?"
"What about her?"
"Apart from the Christmas cards, did she ever write to you again?"

Ted answered from the kitchen, "You must remember she was taking a year out, to tour Europe, I'm sure on that tour I was just one of the many men she met, and then it was back to America to the serious life, to study and to qualify for whatever profession she had decided on. As I said, it was just a fling an enjoyable fling, but nothing more, I guess that's the way with life, we meet, we part, but life goes on, but to answer your question, no she never wrote to me again, she probably doesn't even know I'm back in Ireland. That Christmas card was sent to me in Australia some years after I got there."

Ted brought in the tea, went and got the diaries, and said,
"Now let's have a look."
I said, "You mentioned something about a Paddy O Conner in the pub."
"He was the first Labour mayor of the London Borough of Camden, and first Irish mayor as well, let's wait to see if Tony mentions him, I think we should go through all the notes books first, and then if I remember something, or can add to what's in them, I will; so let's dip in again and see what's on offer."

Chapter Nine

I had only been in London for about two months; I was sharing the second floor in a house down in Queens Park with four other people, two large rooms and a kitchen, two to each room. The person sharing the room with me was from Mayo. O' Mahony was his name I think, Jack or Joe I'm not sure which it was. One thing always stayed in my memory. It was on a Sunday, I had gone to the pictures in the afternoon and came home early and had an early night. My room was facing the street and had two large windows which allowed the amber glow of the street lights into the room, compared to the pitch black darkness of the country it never really gets dark in the city. Sunday was usually a quiet night; most of us sowed our wild oats on Friday or Saturday night and prayed for non fertilisation on Sunday morning.

O' Mahony had gone out for a quiet drink. And at about eleven thirty, I heard voices. It was O'Mahony returning and talking low to someone; and that someone was a woman, and without a doubt she was Irish.

After about twenty minutes they came into the room. I could see their silhouette in the amber glow of the street lights, both of them went to bed, no need to tell you what happened next; suffice to say he didn't bring her back just to sleep with her. Twenty minutes later all was quiet and I fell asleep, only to be awakened by O'Mahony alarm clock at around six.

I'm not sure but I think O'Mahony was one of Murphy's gang, he got up early every morning, he and others went to meet a lorry at some pick up point and got dropped off at various work sites around London. O'Mahony got up and went to the toilet and then back to bed, he was determined to get good value from the woman because he had sex with her again; then got up, dressed himself and went to the bathroom for a wash, then to the kitchen. I could hear him talking to one of the lads who were sharing the room across the landing, I think his name was Eugene, I can't remember his second name. O'Mahony asked him, "How things went last night."

Eugene answered, "I had a quiet night, and anyway I was banjaxed after Saturday night."
O'Mahony said, "No woman then?"
"No nothing doing last night."
"I bet you wouldn't refuse sex now if you got it."

"Would a cat drink milk?"

"I got lucky last night, I met a nice girl and she came home with me, she's still above in the bed, why don't you go up and satisfy yourself."

"What do you mean? You're joking!"

"I'm not joking, why don't you go up and have sex with her, it's still dark, don't say anything and she will think it's me."

"You won't mind?"

"Why should I mind? She's just a one night stand, she'll be gone when I get home tonight I may never see her again."

I heard Eugene come into the room and get into the bed, the woman said nothing, whether she knew it was a different man or not she never let on, I could hear the bed rattling, and Eugene grunting, then silence for a while, and then Eugene rolled over and got out of the bed, I heard the woman pull up the bed clothes and turn on her side.

Some minutes later O' Mahony came into the room and said to the woman, "I have to go to work, you can leave yourself out later; I might see you the week end."

She didn't answer him.

When it was time for me to get up, daylight had replaced the amber light through the window, the woman was faced towards the wall; I could see the back of her head, I closed the bedroom door behind me and went to work.

I decided to move out and get a place of my own, a month later I moved into a small bedsit in West Hampstead.

^

Paul said, "God what sewer did that two ooze out of? You'd think they were sharing a cigarette or a joint, did it really happen?"

"It happened all right, Tony often spoke of it, and it stayed on his mind, he couldn't understand how they could treat a woman like that, or how anyone woman could allow anyone to treat them like that."

I said "God Almighty" why would she allow herself to be cheapened like that; had she any pride, where was her dignity? I'm sure wherever she was brought up in Ireland; she was brought up decent and taught to respect herself."

Ted answered, "I'm sure she was, and then she comes to England and loses all herself respect, why? Why did this happen to a lot of people who went to England? Is it caused by the oppressive narrow minded, and thou shall not attitude of the country they were reared in. Being made feel guilty about everything, and when they escaped from that church controlled guilt ravaged country to an open minded country, where freedom meant freedom, especially freedom of the mind where anything goes, they just can't handle it. And I bet you those two gobshites and the woman were at mass that morning. How fucked up can you be?"

Ted was interrupted by a car horn blowing at his gate. Paul said "That's Mother, coming to pick us up, I guess we have to finish for now."

I said. That's been interesting, and a bit upsetting. I'll call to see you on Monday; I'm looking forward to hearing what else will be revealed."

"Monday it is then lads."

Chapter Ten

I was up early Monday morning and decided to walk to the village for a paper. As I passed Ted's house on my way back from the shop. He shouted, "Come in, and have a cup of tea." He was sitting at a garden table having tea, toast, and marmalade. "Would you like some?" He asked.

"I'll just have a cup of tea, I've had my breakfast."

"I love to sit out here when the weather is good." He poured the tea, saying, "If you were travelling in an unknown country Jim, and you came upon someone having tea toast and marmalade, what would it tell you about that country?"

"I have no idea."

"It would tell you that you were in a civilised country, I think there is nothing more civilised in the world than someone having tea toast and marmalade. And when they sit down to have it, for at least half an hour, everything else in the world should be put completely out of their minds, and their entire concentration should be on the tea toast and marmalade. When I was working Jim, I never had time for a breakfast, out of bed, a coffee and away. Now I make a ritual of breakfast, to make up for all the ones I never had. In the fine mornings I like to sit out here to watch and listen to the sounds of the world.

The sights and sounds of nature, birds singing, butterflies erratically flying from flower to flower, a sheep bleating to a wayward lamb, a cow calling for her calf, waves breaking on the shore, seagulls taking an early morning flight inland for the day. Man made sounds, tractors in the distance tilling the fields, cars on the road, a man shouting at cattle, a boy calling his dog, a mother calling her children. Sights and sounds I never had time to observe or listen to before, now as the song says *I have all the time in the world*. Why should I have to die to experience heaven, when I have heaven here, and I'm alive to enjoy it?"
"You make it sound so wonderful, I'm sorry for interrupting you."
"Not to mind Jim, just don't make a habit of it; anyway it's nice to have company for a change."

I asked, "Do you think Paul is right?"
"What is he right about?"
"Do you remember the first time I mentioned the poem? He asked does it matter anymore, he said it's so long ago; it's all in the past. Whether there's a story or not, should we let it be?"

"A hundred years, a thousand, or one million years Jim, it makes no difference; everything that happened in the past has brought us here to this very moment, the present! And that is all the present is, a fleeting second, what I said a second ago is now in the past. As for the future, we have no guarantee of that, no memories of it, as far as we are concerned it has not yet existed, and for some it never will. So all we are sure of is the past, ninety nine per cent of our lives is the past. Whatever we have done, what we got right, what we got wrong, people we knew, relations, friends, enemies, all in the past, and all stored in our mind, a D V D of our life to be turned on whenever we want to. I for one think it is worth remembering, and delving into it."

"People say Ted that we should learn from our past, mistakes that were made should not be repeated."
"Everyone makes mistakes Jim, it is part of life, but when we realise we have made a mistake, we should learn from it, try and put it right, but some things cannot be rightified. But we should insure they won't happen again. I think the poem is interesting, and some of it is true it recalls events that happened back then, maybe it is a long time ago, but it is history, it tells a story, someone wrote it. So I think why not you, Paul, and I try and learn that story. You were very enthusiastic at the beginning, have you changed your

mind?"

"No, I, it's, I just that I don't want to be pestering you and taking up your time."

"I'm enjoying it, and as I have already said, I have all the time in the world, and it's bringing back good memories of places and friends I once knew, and you are hoping to make your mark as a writer, so if pursuing these diaries leads to a short story for your paper, or a longer story for yourself, it may help you to fulfil that ambition, why not continue?"

"I just wanted to make sure that you want to continue."

"I certainly do Jim, I certainly do."

"All right then, Paul and I will call around this evening."

"When are you going back to London?"

"As I said my editor gave me a week here, to see if I can conjure up something to write about. I can go back anytime during the week, but I must be at my desk by Monday morning."

"Paul is working all week Jim, I think if we are to make any headway you and I will have to spend most of the week going through the diaries without Paul, if we are to make any progress we have to get on with it."

"I don't want to go back to London without finding something out, I want to know by the end of the week whether I have a story or not, I can explain to Paul. I'm sure he'll understand I can fill him in on what's happening, so you go get the diaries Ted and let's make a start."

Ted went and got the diaries came back, and said, "Right let's drop in on Tony and company again."

Seven thirty on a warm July evening I was walking towards the Swiss Cottage pub to meet with Ben Mason. As well as his library job Ben worked now and then as a doorman in some of the clubs, and tonight he was working in a club in the west end, and he had asked me if I would go with him. He told me I could make a nice few quid working the clubs, and said he would show me the ropes. As I entered the pub, Ben shouted, "Up this end Tony."

I joined him at the bar. He asked, "What's your poison?"

"I'll have a light and bitter; tell me, do you think I'll be able for this door work."

"No bother Tony, after a few nights you'll get the hang of it, I'll be with you and show you who to let in, and who to keep an eye on."

"What time must we be there?"

"We'll have another pint here, and then hop on a bus, there's a nice pub across from the club, we can have one there before we go on duty."

"Sounds good to me," And I called for two more drinks.

A t nine o clock Ben and I were on duty at the club door. Ben knew most of the people who entered and he bantered with them. Ben had spent his early years around this part of London so he knew most of them, he named some of them, knew what they did for a living. Some were hard working business men out for the night, some in show business. Others were a bit on the shady side, making their living from things that fell off the back of Lorries. Ben hung around with shady people in his early years, not that he did anything wrong, he just knew some of them, then he was conscripted, shipped overseas for a few years, did his tour of duty, was then demobbed and walked the straight and narrow ever since.

I had met him for the first time in a little pub called the Winchester in Swiss cottage. I was having a quiet pint there when a loud mouthed drunk started to abuse a black South African who was a regular; I interfered and told to him to leave him be. I was about to get flattened, when I heard someone say, "I wouldn't do that if I were you mate," And Ben stepped between us. The drunk backed off. Ben introduced himself saying, "Irish by your accent, I'm Ben, London and cockney, so we have a few things in common."

"Glad to meet you, very glad as a matter of fact, I'm
Tony Powel, you came to my rescue there, but I don't
know what we have in common."

"How to enjoy life", he answered. "We know how to
celebrate, whether it's a birth, marriage, or death, we
like a knees up. Let me get you a pint, what's you
poison?"

"I'll have a light and bitter."

These thoughts were going through my mind while
keeping an eye on the punters coming and going.

Then Ben said, "Will you be okay on your own for a few
minutes, I must go shake hands with my best friend."

I had a puzzled look on my face.

So he said, "The jax, I must go to the jax, I'll be back in a
few minutes."

Two men and two women approached the club door; it
was plain to see that the two women had a lot of drink
on board. I blocked their entrance to the club saying,
"Sorry patrons only."

One of the men said, "Who the fuck do you think you
are? We are patrons, now step to fuck aside and let us
in."

I held my position.

One of the women said, "Show him whose boss around

here." Just as they were about to push their way in, I heard Ben shout, "Tony, Tony, it's okay, it's okay." Ben stepped between us, "Saying, hold it, hold, back off, it's his first night, he's just learning."

One of the men said, "Tell him Ben, if that ever happens again, his learning days are over, and all other kind of days as well."

"It won't happen; now in you go and enjoy yourself."

Christ Ben said "You picked on a right pair there."

"Who are they?"

"Who are they? You have just been talking to the Kray brothers."

^

I interrupted Ted's reading, saying "You knew the Kray Brothers?" The most notorious gangsters in London back then.

"No, not really Jim, I heard of them, Ben knew them before his army days; Tony never met them again after that night at the club."

"There's still no mention of Christine Arkwright, or whatever name she wrote under, will he mention her at all."

"Knowing Tony, and how he felt about Christine I have no doubt he will mention her. Remember in his letter he said he would deal with things in a random kind of way. I think it was around sixty four when they first met. I'll go and refill the teapot before we get back to the diaries."

As we were about to delve into the diaries again a voice from behind said? "Doing a bit of reading in the sunshine?"

"A bit of reminiscing Biddy, talking of old friends and times past," Ted introduced her saying, "My neighbour Biddy Murphy, Biddy this is Jim Clarke."

I said, "Glad to meet you" and recognised her as the woman who gave Ted the lift home from the pub the night he sang the song.

Biddy said, "I know who it is, sure don't I know his mother well."

I asked Biddy, "Did you ever hear of someone called Tony Powell around here?"

"Tony Powell? Let me see now, Tony... Powell? No, sorry, no, can't help you there, he's not living around here; if he was I would have heard of him, Tony Powell? No he's definitely not from around here. I'm going shopping Ted, do you want anything?"

"Thanks Biddy, I do need a few things. A bit of stewing beef, a piece of bacon and some mince meat."

Biddy said, "No bother I'll see you later."

"Wait until I go in for some money."

"You can pay me when I get back," And she was gone as quick as she had come.

"She looks after you well."
"She's a good friend and neighbour."
"And that's it Ted?"
"Now Jim don't go putting two and two together and getting six, just friends nothing more."
"As long as Biddy is around you won't go hungry."
"Enough for the week, I'll get two days from the stew, reheat it the second day, two days from the bacon, hot the first day, and cold the next, shepherd's pie from the mince, two days from that as well, and I'll eat out on Sunday."
"You have it all well planned".
Ted picking up the diaries said, "You can't beat a bit of planning; now let's open this doorway to the sixties and see what Tony Powell has planned.

Chapter Eleven

It was one o clock on a Saturday afternoon. I was sitting in a quiet corner of the Swiss Cottage Pub, drinking a pint of light and bitter and eating a plate of sausages and mash when Ben joined me, I asked "What are you having?"

"A pint of bitter will do just fine, the sausages and mash looks good, I'll have some of that, and you stay where you are, I'll get it, and what are you drinking?"

"I'll have a light and bitter."

Ben came back with the drinks and the mash, saying "When we have these finished; we'll be on our way."

"What's the hurry it's only one o clock, the match don't start 'till three."

"We need to go a bit earlier today, any time Man Utd is at the bridge, they bring a big crowd, once we have our tickets we can have a pint or two inside."

"Do you think Ben that Chopper Harris can handle Georgie boy?"

"I hate to say it, but I think two or three Choppers wouldn't handle him."

"What are our chances?"

"I think Tony; if they hadn't Best we would have some chance, who knows with a bit of luck, maybe!"

Half an hour later we were sitting on a number thirty one bus on our way to Chelsea and Stamford Bridge. We got into one of the queues for tickets, and slowly made our way to the turnstile. It was a dry cold November day, a light north east wind blowing; it would be a cold day sitting in the stand. We eventually got to our seats. I went and got two coffees, handed one to Ben and said, "It's too cold for beer." And we waited for the match to start.

It was a great game, the two teams trying hard to win. Ten minutes to go and no score, then George Best showed his genius, receiving the ball on the halfway line he took on the entire Chelsea defence, left Chopper for dead, rounded the goalkeeper Peter Bonetti, and tapped the ball into the net. The Man Utd fans erupted, even some of the Chelsea fans cheered, it was so brilliant. That's the way it ended, one nil to Utd. The crowds streamed away from Stamford Bridge.
Ben said, "We have no hope of getting a bus with this crowd, come on he said follow me; we'll slip down this side street; there's a quiet pub off the beaten track; we'll have a couple of pints, and when it quietens down we'll get the bus to Swiss Cottage."

Ben went to the bar ordered two pints of bitter, I found an empty table, and Ben came back with the drinks. "Cheers" I said, "Taking a swig."

Ben said, "It's quiet in here."
I looked around the bar. A few people sitting at tables, two or three men at one end of the counter, a woman at the other end was sipping a coffee and had a guitar slung over her shoulder and a flower in her hair, "Looks like we've got a pop star here" I said.
Ben looked around and asked, "Where?"
I said, "There" Pointing to the counter, "she's a stunner."
"She sure is."

I went to the counter for two more pints, deliberately standing next to the girl with the guitar, as the barman was filling the pints, I said, "Any chance of a tune".
She answered, "Not right now, but if I were to sing I suppose you would want *Glory, Glory Man Utd*."
"What makes you think that?"
"They were playing at the Bridge" she answered.
"I know, I was at the match, but if you were to sing me a team song, I'd prefer *Blue is the Colour*."
"You! A Chelsea fan, I don't believe it."
"And may I ask why not?"
"I thought your accent; being Irish you would support

Man Utd."

"We don't all *peel em and eat em and follow the crowd.*"

"Sorry I shouldn't assume things."

"I forgive you this time; can I get you a drink?"

"No thanks; I just came in for a coffee, just to let the football crowd disperse."

Ben came to the counter, "A man could die of thirst around here." he said.

"Sorry, I was talking to this lady here, I would introduce her, but I don't know her name."

"Christine Arkwright" she said.

"I'm Tony Powell, this is Ben Mason."

She shook hands with me, then Ben.

"Were you at the match," I asked her.

"No, I was at an anti war rally, Peace not war is the way."

I asked, "the flower in your hair, is it a sign of peace?"

"Yes, a symbol of peace and harmony. We were protesting against the war in Vietnam, trying to persuade L. B. J to pull out."

"That will take a lot of persuading. I wonder if J. F. K had survived would it make any difference."

"I don't know, maybe, who can say?"

"I wonder who was behind his shooting".

She answered, "Oswald and Ruby weren't alone,

Kennedy's death goes straight to the top, I think Ruby shot Oswald so he wouldn't talk, and then he was shot for the same reason."

"So many theories, I answered, maybe someday as they say, *it will all come out in the wash.*"

Ben said, "We better be going Tony, I need to get back and get changed and go for something to eat."

"Where are you going to eat?"

"I might try that Indian restaurant in Finchley road."

"It's good, I had a meal there last week," and then I said to Christine, "We have to go."

Christine said, "I heard your friend mention Finchley road, do you live near there?"

"I live in West Hampstead."

"You're not too far from me, I live in Belsize Park, we have a second hand book shop there and a printing business, when I say we, I mean my parents."

"I know it; I often pass there, and now that I know where you live; I have no doubt we'll meet again."

"I hope so, when you're passing why not call in? I might sell you a book or two."

I'll be looking forward to that."

Ben said, I'm sorry to interrupt you two, but I think it's time to catch that bus."

I turned at the door and waved to Christine, she waved back.

On the bus I said to Ben, "Isn't she the most beautiful person you ever saw, do you believe in love at first sight. Now I know how Shakespeare could write, *shall I compare thee to a summer's day?* Or why John Keats wrote, *Bright Star. Pillowed upon my fair love's ripening breast/to feel forever its soft swell and fall/Awake forever in sweet unrest /Still, still to hear her tender taken – breath/and so live forever or swoon to death.* "Can you imagine that Ben?"

"You bet I can, and I am, especially the part about being pillowed upon her breast, but it's harder to imagine you quoting Keats. In God's name tell me, where you got that from?"

"I went for a walk on the heath a few weeks ago, on my way there I passed Keats house and decided to call in. It was a wonderful experience, a house and garden of tranquillity in the middle of a growling city. When you step through the portal, it's not a step into a house, but a step from the twenty first century to the nineteenth, you should visit it someday. Then I went into the library next door, joined, and took out a book of Keats poems, and I've been reading them on and off ever since."

∧

Leaving down the diaries, Ted said, "I guess from the first time he saw her Cupid struck him right between the two eyes and pole axed him, are you happy now? He's mentioned Christine at last?"

"I think Ted without a doubt she had an effect on him."

"An effect Jim, that's putting it mildly, he was obsessed with her. His whole life changed the day he met her, from the time he got up in the morning until he went to bed at night he lived for nothing else. He left London because of her, and wherever he went, or whatever he did after that, I have no doubt he always thought of her and still does to this day. I haven't met Tony since he left London but I'd be willing to bet with anyone that he never married."

"You mean he's spent his entire life wandering the world obsessed with one woman. That's sad."

"Oh I'm sure he had other woman, I'm sure he was in love with other women, but not as he loved Christine; all just passing fancies, substitutes for the real thing, Christine is stored forever in his mind and will remain there."

"Do you still have hope of finding out the name Christine is writing under?"

"I don't know Jim these diaries are all about the sixties. Christine was known then only to her friends as a writer, if she did achieve success it was later on, and under a different name.

"I know Ted they're all about the sixties, but maybe in them, somewhere, some clue..."

"I doubt it Jim as I said the other day, I only ever heard Tony refer to her as Christine, unless back then she submitted some of her poems to the papers under a different name, if she did, maybe she used that name in later years, maybe in conversations with him she mentions that name, and hopefully he might mention it in the diaries, but even without knowing that name you will still get a story from the diaries, or at least an article for your paper."

"I guess you're right Ted, so let's continue."

"Right so; I'll make a fresh pot of tea, and then using the diaries as a time machine let us travel back once more.

Chapter Twelve

On Sunday night I was working on the presses down in
Fleet St until three in the morning, so I didn't get to bed
until four, and got up at 11 30, washed and shaved,
went to a nearby cafe for breakfast, got a window seat
and sat for a while watching the world go by. It was a
typical dry cold cloudy November day and I had the
afternoon to myself. And as I had Christine on my mind
since I met her, I knew the first thing I was going to do
was walk to Belsize Park and call to the book shop to
see if she was there. Half an hour later I was standing
outside it, reading a part time help wanted sign in the
window.

Then Christine came out and said; "Nice to see you
again, are you applying for the job?"
"If I do will you hire me?"
"That's my Fathers decision, but maybe I could influence
him."
"Why part time?" I asked.
"I work here most days, but I spend a lot of time in the
print room, writing and printing my poems and
pamphlets, and printing for father and the public. I'm
often away on demos, and Father travels a lot, to book

fairs, always in search of that rare book; so someone part time would be a great help."

"You're a poet as well as a singer, multi talented."

"Poetry and writing are my big passion, my dream is to have a novel published someday, and singing is my second passion, I often put a tune to my poems and sing them at demos and when I'm busking."

"Only two passions: what about love and romance?"

"Not at the moment, love and romance are not within my radar at present. I mean serious love, the kind that ties you down. With most of your time taking up with meeting each other, and going here and going there, you can't fulfil your goals in life. And before you know it, talks of marriage and family. That's not for me, well not right now anyway. Maybe an odd date, dinner with someone with mutual interests, no strings attached, anything serious will have to wait until sometime in the future, at least until I've succeeded, or failed in my ambition."

"No point in asking you to marry me then."

Christine laughed and said, "No definitely not, not at the moment, ask again in about twenty years."

"About the job, I work part time in Fleet Street on the printing presses, part time here would suit me, and I could help with the printing as well."

"Father's not here now, could you come back tomorrow and you can be officially interviewed."

A customer came to the counter to ask about a book.

Christine said, "I'll be with you in a minute; I must go now, hope to see you tomorrow."

"I have no doubt you will, bye for now."

On the way past Swiss Cottage Library I called in to see Ben.

"I was hoping I'd see you mate he said, I've got a job lined up for us tonight, down west, some up and coming band are playing a gig there, they're expecting a large crowd; a lot of screaming teenagers, are you up for it?"

"Sure Ben, no bother the extra cash will come in handy."

"Okay then, we'll meet me in the Swiss Cottage around eight."

The pub was quiet when I walked in, the evening punters gone home, the late night ones hadn't arrived yet. Ben called for two light and bitters.

"Now then tell me more about this gig, no Kray brothers I hope."

"No worries Tony, no Kray brothers, just some up and coming band, supposed to be the next big thing. The manager of the club wants a few of us to stand in front of the stage, to keep the crowd from getting up there."

"Seems handy enough, what time will it finish."
"Not too late; remember some of the crowd are as young as sixteen."

The main act came on at 9 30, Ben and I and about half a dozen more stewards, were lined across the front of the stage. The M C said; "Let's give a wonderful London reception to the next world sensation, ladies and gentlemen we are proud to bring to you, *The Beatles*." The place erupted in a screaming mass of hysterical teenagers, as four young mop headed lads started to play. We had to call for reinforcements as the crowd surged towards the stage, they were shaking, screaming, crying, dancing, some fainted, we had to lift them on to front of the stage to keep them from being trampled on.
Two hours later the band played their last song and Ben and I made sure they got to their dressing room safely.

"Thanks guys they said, come in a minute."
A few forty fives were on the dressing table, the drummer said, "Here have a couple of these." He took a pen from a drawer, and wrote *thanks from the Beatles,* and he signed *Ringo*, the other three signed, *John, Paul, George*.
"Did you enjoy the gig?" Paul asked.
I answered, "Great and it's nice to be able to hear the

words, with some bands you can't hear the words with the noise they make."

He said, "Not much point in writing or singing a song if the words can't be heard."

I said, "True, and thanks for the forty fives."

We went back to the hall and the manager payed us, and remarked, "You certainly earned your money tonight, what are your thoughts on the band?"

Ben answered, "They're not Elvis, Buddy Holly, or Chuck Berry, but the youngsters liked them; they might have a future."

I said, "With the hair style they have, they are like four mop heads, but I must say they had me moving to the beat, and if a band can set the body in motion, that's a good sign."

At eleven o clock the following morning I was standing in the book shop talking to Christine.

She said, "Father's in the print room; he'll be with you soon."

A few minutes later he came through the door of the print room, I guessed he was about six feet, in his forties, a good head of hair that once was fair, but now sprinkled with grey.

Christine said, "Dad, this is Tony Powell, and he's come about the job."

He offered me his hand, and said, "Glad to meet you,

I'm Harry Arkwright," and in an accent that wasn't quite upper class, but almost."

"I'm Tony Powell, I'm interested in the Job."

"Would a part time job suit you?" He asked.

I answered, "At the moment I'm working on the printing presses down in Fleet Street, that's kind of part time, it's not always guaranteed they'll call you in, I also do some door work at night."

"Door work... what kind of door work?"

"In the clubs, and halls keeping things under control, I was working last night at a venue down the west end, trying to keep a mob of frenzied teenagers from a pop group called the Beatles."

Christine said, "You saw the Beatles last night? And then she sang... *she loves you yeah, yeah, yeah*, "that's fantastic."

"You've heard of them?"

"Of course I've heard of them, and the whole world will soon hear of them."

I took one of the forty five's they had given us from my pocket; "Here, you have this."

"They gave you this?"

They gave us two; my mate Ben has the other one."

"They've signed it! Wonderful and she kissed me on the cheek.

Her father said, "You have two jobs already?"

"I do, but the hours don't clash, and if you were to hire me, I could manage this as well."

"But would a full time job suit you better?"

"Not really, too regimental, nine to five, eight to whatever, too tied down, this way I work different hours, my time off varies, it gives me a sense of freedom, and I like it that way."

He said, "I have no doubt you could do this job, Christine, what do you think?"

She answered, with a mischievous smile on her face, "Give him a week's trial and if he doesn't suit, you can sack him then."

"My, my, that's a bit drastic, but I do need someone, it may as well be you as anybody else, can you start on Monday?"

"Thank you, I can."

"Then the job is yours, welcome on board," and he went to attend to a customer.

"Dad it's not too busy at the moment; I'll take a quick break."

Christine followed me out, "Saying there's a nice little cafe across the street. Will you join me for a coffee?"

"Delighted to, and I'll buy; just to say thanks for your help."

The cafe was quiet, waiting for the lunch crowd to come in.

"Will you have something to eat," I asked.

"No thanks, just a coffee."

I ordered two coffees, took them to a table, Christine was reading the cover of the forty five.

"I can't believe you met the Beatles, they're fantastic, a revolution in the music world."

"All part of the nights work, are you working on Monday?"

"I am... I'm not working Saturday, so I'll have to work Monday."

"Good, it will be nice to be greeted by a friendly face."

"Do you think my father's not friendly then?

"Yes, yes of course he is, a lovely man, I mean it will be nice to see you again."

"You can see me before Monday that's if you want to."

I wanted to answer, right now that's what I want more than anything else in the world, but asked, "Would you like to go out with me on Friday night."

"No not Friday night she answered, I'm up very early on Saturday morning."

"But you just said you're not working on Saturday."

"I meant not working in the shop, there's a big peace rally in Trafalgar Sq on Saturday, if you want to see me before Monday you could call to the book shop on Friday afternoon and help me print some posters, and on Saturday come to the rally with me."

"I'll come to the book shop and give you a hand on Friday; I'm not too sure about Saturday."

"Why? Don't you believe in peace?"

"Of course I believe in peace, live and let live is my motto, but a protest march here in London, is that going to impress L B J?"

"If the world protests he will have to listen."

"I had planned to watch Chelsea at Spurs on Saturday."

"What's more important? What's happening in Vietnam, or twenty two grown men chasing after a ball?"

"When you put it like that, what can I say? All right I'll come with you on Saturday."

"Good, call at around three on Friday and we'll work on the posters."

I walked back to the shop with her and said, "See you on Friday."

I walked into the book shop at ten to three on Friday afternoon; Christine's father was behind the counter browsing through a book, he looked up and said, "Tony Powell isn't it? You don't start work until Monday."

"I know; I've come to help Christine with some pamphlets for the rally tomorrow."

"Oh, oh, I see. I'm just browsing through the poems of a fellow countryman of yours, *W B Yeats,* and I can highly recommend his poetry to you."

I asked him, "Do you prefer the old poems or the poems of today."

He answered "Old poems do not exist, old poets yes, but there are no old poems. The poems of a bygone age are as fresh and as relevant to the first time readers of today as they were to the readers who first encountered them two or three hundred years ago, poetry transcends time, poetry nourishes the soul. It's the bible of the enlightened, only through poetry can the definitive vision of a happening be revealed to the mind", then he said, "Christine's in the print room, go straight through."

"Which door?"

"The one on the right, the other one is to our private quarters."

I said, "Thanks" and walked in to the print room.

Christine was at a table working on some posters, her hair tied in a pony tail, a smudge of ink on her cheek, and a loose strand of hair between her ear and nose. She was the kind of woman who didn't have to dress up, or put on make up to look beautiful, it just came natural to her, and I stood inside the door for a few seconds admiring her.

"Are you going to just stand there, or come over here and lend a hand?"

"How can I help?"

"That poster I've just typed up, can you take it over to the copying machine and make twenty copies."

"Sure no bother," I read the poster, *Peace, not war, troops out.* Some of Christine's poems were on the table near the copying machine, as the machine was copying, I picked up one. "Do you mind if I read this?"

"Not at all, that's why we write poems, in the hope that someone will read them."

"It was called *Permanent Tear.* I finished the poem and said, "You're good."

"Tell that to some of the publishers and newspapers who've turned me down, that one is going to be a song, I just must put a tune to it."

"I suppose some of your poems are anti establishment, and they don't want to upset the status quo; you condemn what they are in favour of, they can see changes are coming and they are afraid of those changes. They don't want to change their ways, they won't be told what to do by teenagers, radical poets, beatniks, and especially by people who wear flowers in their hair, and they can't understand that."

"Flowers in our hair are just a symbol of peace, a symbol of harmony."

"Most of the leaders in the world today Christine would rather spread mayhem than harmony; love, peace and harmony to them is just namby – pamby, they are more comfortable making war instead of love."

"What did you say?"

I said "Most of the leaders in the world today would rather spread mayhem than harmony"...

"No not that, something about war and love."

I said, "They'd rather make war instead of love?

Christine said, "That's great, that's great, turn it around and we have a wonderful slogan", *Make love not war.*

"I'll type that up and make some posters, and we are not anti establishment. We are anti something's, not everything. We are anti apartheid, anti war, and in your own country, the Republic and Northern Ireland, in both those place the Catholics and the Protestant should have equal rights. If a Government cannot provide equal rights for all its citizen, then that Government is a failure, they call us communists; I am not a communist; but if believing that every citizen is entitled to his dignity and equal status in his own country, if that makes me a communist, then I would be proud to be one."

For the next hour and a half we worked on posters and hand outs for the rally.

Then Christine said, "I think we have enough, some of the other organisers are making some as well."

"What time are you going tomorrow?" I asked her.

"Meet me here at around ten. Dad said he'll drive us down, if we get there around eleven that should give us plenty of time to get organised."

I asked her, "Is your organisation the only one protesting tomorrow, any hawks, any pro Vietnam?"

"I'm sure some groups will be there, but we don't want any trouble, just a peaceful demonstration."

"I have no doubt that's what you want, but trouble is second nature to some people."

Are you sure Christine you don't want to come for a drink with me?"

"No thanks, I'm working on an air for that poem you just read, if the papers won't publish it, then I can bring it to the attention of the public by singing it, and I must change the first line of a song I intend to sing tomorrow, I want to include the words, *Make love, not war*"

"Okay I'll see you tomorrow then."

"How are you going to spend your evening?"

"I'll see if Ben and a few of the boys are in the Winchester or Swiss Cottage, have a bite to eat and a few drinks, I'll see you in the morning then."

"See you, bye."

Ben was in the Swiss Cottage when I got there.

"What have you been up to?" He asked.

"I was preparing for a peace rally tomorrow in Trafalgar Square."

"What? You! On a peace rally; I thought we were going to White Hart Lane for Spurs and Chelsea."

"I've changed my mind."

"What's come over you? You! Going to a peace rally instead of a soccer match, are you losing your marbles?"

"No, it's a matter of getting our priorities right, a choice of watching twenty two men chasing a bag of wind around a field, or doing something for mankind."

"Well, I never, I'm gobsmacked, you concerned about the benefit of mankind? I thought the only concern you had right now is who you are going to take to bed tonight, and getting up in time for the match tomorrow, I have no doubt this is not all about a peace rally, a woman is involved here, and that woman's name is Christine".

The barman asked, "And who is Christine?"

Ben answered, "A young woman, we met in a pub in Chelsea after the last match."

The barman said, "She's a Chelsea supporter?"

"No she was on a peace rally that day, she just popped in for a coffee to avoid the crowd and she wears a flower in her hair, writes poetry and sings protest songs."

"A beatnik..." The barman said, "You're involved with a

beatnik."

I answered, "She is not a beatnik, she is a very responsible young woman who is very concerned about what's happening in Vietnam, and is willing to do something about it and the under privileged in this world. A flower in her hair doesn't make her a beatnik; the flower is just a symbol of peace. She doesn't go around every day with a flower in her hair, she wears it at an odd rally; Christine works hard, in her book shop, at her poetry and song writing. She takes what she does seriously, if there were more young people like her in the world, it might be a better place for everyone to live in."

Ben said, "Blimey mate whatever she is, I think we need to take you to a doctor, the Spurs and Chelsea match is going to be a cracker tomorrow, and you are willing to miss that, just to go on a rally with a crowd of tree huggers."

The barman said, "I don't think it's the trees he wants to hug, but Christine."

Ben said "Hells bells mate this is getting out of hand, I know she's a good looking girl and all that, but to miss the Spurs and Chelsea match for a peace rally, cor blimey mate you're off your rocker, if you think a peace rally is better than a good soccer match, you are deluded."

"Blessed are the deluded Ben, they shall not have to confront reality."

"Nip it in the bud right now Tony before it's too late, Trafalgar Sq tomorrow? And walking down the aisle in twelve months time, life as you know it, over and done with, on no account can you go to that rally tomorrow, it's White Hart Lane or ruination."

"I have no intention of walking down the aisle, just because you're friends with a woman, that doesn't mean you are going to marry her, anyway Christine is not the marrying type."

"That's what you think mate, all women are the marrying type."

"Not Christine, she's a writer, a poet, a musician, she wants to achieve something in life, make a name for herself, and do something for the benefit of mankind and she's not going to give up that dream for an apron and a pram."

"Have it your way Tony but wait and see, it's a woman's natural instinct to marry, and I guarantee Christine is no exception."

"Christine is one of a kind Ben, and she will do what she wants to do, now what are you having?"

"Thanks mate I think I'll have a gin and tonic I'm

suffering from shock, and as they say, *Feck the expense, give the cat a gold fish.*"

Chapter Thirteen

At ten o clock on Saturday morning I was knocking on Christine's door. She was almost ready to go. But first she offered me a cup of tea and had one herself. Her father backed the car out of the garage, a Hillman estate. Christine and I loaded all the placards and posters, and at eleven o clock we were on our way. Christine was in front with her father, I was in the back with Christine's guitar standing on the seat beside me. Her father asked, "Will it be alright if I drop you in Charing Cross Rd, I don't want to get caught in the crowd."

"That will do fine dad, Tony and I will manage from there."

There was quite a lot of traffic, and no parking space to be found. Harry said, "I'll have to double park here, Christine you and Tony unload quickly before a traffic warden comes along."

We unloaded as fast as we could, and Harry drove off and we stood on the sidewalk with all our paraphernalia. "Now what"... I asked.

"Walk to Nelson's Column." Christine answered and picked up her guitar and some posters, I gathered the rest and we joined the crowd walking towards Trafalgar Square. The square was thronged, mostly young people, and some tourists taking photographs. Some of the women wore kaftans and others wore light colourful ankle length dresses and sandals, some had garlands of flowers in their hair and beads around their necks, their faces painted with flowers and various other emblems. The *all Seeing Eye* observed the event from several foreheads. The men wore loose fitting various coloured shirts and tops over flared bottom trousers or jeans, most of them wore moccasins, the smell of hashish drifted on the air.

Music from hundreds of transistors radios rocked the Square, the Beatles, the Rolling Stones, the Cream, the Small Faces and the Mamas and Papas. On a radio near me I could hear Scott McKenzie singing *San Francisco*. When the song finished the D J referred to it as the Anthem for flower power.
Nearly everyone had a placard or poster with slogans on them, some had pictures of L B J and *warmonger* on the same poster; I distributed Christine's posters *Make love, not war.*

A make shift stage was erected near Nelson's Column for the main speakers; the police were mingling and keeping a watchful eye on everyone and everything.

Each speaker took the stage to loud cheering and shouting, then a few people shouted *make love, not war* and soon thousands of people took up the chant around Trafalgar Square.

Christine climbed on to the stage and was introduced as a poet and songwriter, I only heard the first two lines of her song, *make love, not war and the world will be a better place to live / maybe just a sign of peace and harmony is what we all should give.* Then the square erupted again with the chant. *Make love, not war... Make love, not war... Make love, not war.*

One of the organisers appealed for silence. In the brief period of silence that followed I could hear shouting coming from the Mall. About four hundred people were converging on Trafalgar Sq, wearing leather jackets and jeans with large turn ups, most of them sporting Mohican haircuts and shouting down with communism, reds out, bomb them now.

I could also hear the sirens of extra police cars. I thought to myself this could turn nasty; scuffles had already started at the edge of the crowd. I kicked the placard off the piece of timber I was holding and made my way towards the stage. Some of the anti peace people had already been among the crowd and were now causing mayhem. The police were losing the battle to keep order; they were hopelessly outnumbered having completely underestimated the size of the crowd.

I used the piece of timber in my hand to force my way to the stage. Christine and some of the organisers were still up there. The police had formed a barrier across in front of it, and it was just a matter of time before the crowd swept them aside. I made my way around to the back, and above the din I tried to get Christine's attention. She eventually heard me; I took her guitar and I helped her down.

I said, "Stay close to me, most of the trouble is at the Mall end, we'll try to go towards Charing Cross Rd." With the handle of my placard in one hand and the guitar in the other we pushed our way through the crowd. We were confronted by two leather clad war mongers.

"Commie lovers, fucking commie lovers," one of them said. The other one said, "Let's kick the crap out of them."

Now I'm not a violent man; but sometimes you have to act on your instincts, and my instincts were telling me right now to pull as hard as I could with the timber I had in my hand. I handed the guitar to Christine and taking the placard handle in both hands I aimed for his chest, he raised his hand automatically to protect himself; I made contact with his wrist, I swung again across his knee and as he leaned forward I met him under the jaw with a right upper cut. The other war monger turned and ran. And then I shouter at Christine..."Come on let's get out of here." We reached Charing Cross Rd, which was packed with people in a panic trying to get away.

We walked and ran, eventually reaching Tottenham Court Rd, which was relatively quiet compared to the mayhem we had left behind, the farther we walked the quieter it got, at the top end of the road was what seemed to be a quiet enough pub.

I said, "I don't know about you, but I could do with a drink."

"A cup of coffee and a sit down would be wonderful" she answered.

It was quiet at the counter; I asked the barman for a double whiskey and water, and a cup of coffee.

With an Irish accent he asked, "Do you want Scotch or the real thing."

"I'll have the real thing, a Jameson if you have it?"

"A Jameson it is then."

I added a small amount of water to the whiskey and joined Christine at the table.

"I don't understand what happened she said, and who were these people? And where did you learn to defend yourself like that."

I answered, "It wasn't *on the playing fields of Eton*, but on the hurling grounds of Waterford, and they were an anti peace mob. Not everyone wants America to withdraw from Vietnam; they view a victory there as a victory against communism."

Christine sighed and said; "If people could walk the middle line the world would be a more peaceful place. Extremes in politics, in religion, extremes in anything have caused so much trouble down through the ages, people determined to kill for their beliefs and force them on other people; anyone who kills in the name of their God are putting that God to shame."

"Everyone looks at it differently Christine, some people think your rally today was forcing your message on other people."

"Maybe, but that message was intended to be conveyed peacefully, until people decided to use violence to oppose it, violence is an ignorant weapon, used by ignorant people."

"You could be right, but you must admit it's been a very successful weapon down through the ages. When it comes to obtaining power, turning the other cheek has not been as successful as a fist in the teeth."

"It's all so disheartening, will war ever end? What will satisfy the war mongers? The destruction of the world! What in God's name is stopping people living in peace together? God all mighty what's wrong with the human race? Look at South Africa, over half their population condemned to live as second class citizens and slaves, and the southern states of America; racism, the vicious, violent Ku Klux Klan, and the Mississippi Governor barring a young a black man from university. He's not barring him from joining the army and dying in Vietnam; why would anyone want to die for a country that treats them like that."

"It is indeed Christine a strange and violent world and I have no answers. The song you wrote for today, what with all the noise I only heard the first two lines, what's it about?"

"It's about more or less what we've been talking about; extremes, war, religion."

"Can I hear it?"

"I won't sing it, I'll recite it."

"That will do just fine."

Make love, not war and the world will be a better place to live / maybe a sign of peace and harmony is what we all should give. This earth is, oh so small, when compared to the universe for size/ but we must learn to share it, rich and poor, the foolish and the wise.

*All Christians, Jews and Muslims believe their God is
right / and then they try to prove it, with mayhem death
and might. You are right to revere your God, and to
believe he's the best / but you have no right to force
that belief on me and all the rest. I believe our Gods are
peaceful, but we put those Gods to shame / when we
cause death and carnage, and we cause it in their name.
I'm sure you must have noticed as they gathered up the
dead / the victims, though of different creed and colour,
all their blood ran red. And whatever is your colour,
whether, yellow, white or black / your skin is just the
wrapping and you cannot give it back.*

2

*If I could find a peace dust, I'd climb a mountain high /
and there I'd cast it to the wind and stand and watched
it fly. And as it blew around the earth, it would bring war
to an end / spreading peace and harmony and turning
foe to friend. But I cannot find a peace dust, I know
that's just a dream / so peace and understanding must
come by other means.
Are our Gods that different? Or is it the human race /
who cannot accept each other's politics, creed and face.
What if I were to tell you? Our Gods are from the same
large tree / and sprouting from the one trunk, a branch
for you and me. So make love, not war and the world*

will be a better place to live / maybe a sign of peace and harmony is what we all should give. This earth is, oh so small, when compared to the universe for size / but we must learn to share it, rich and poor, the foolish and the wise.

"That's powerful stuff Christine."

"Even if it is, will it make any difference, who will listen?"

"We can only hope that someday peace will break out. Do you want another coffee?"

"I don't think so, no thanks, I think we should go."

"Tell you what let's get a taxi back to Swiss Cottage; there's a nice little cafe there where we can get something to eat."

"I don't know, I should go home, mum and dad will be concerned about me, what happened at the rally will surely be on the news."

"There's a phone box outside the door, ring them; let them know your okay, and then after we've eaten I'll walk you home."

Christine looked at me with a question mark on her face, and then said, "All right."

^

Ted dropped the diaries on to the table, rubbed his eyes and said to Jim, "Now that you've got to know Christine better, what do you think?"

"What I'm thinking right now is those two Beatles forty fives must be worth a fortune if there still around, imagine! One of their first records and signed by the four of them."

"Worth thousands I'd say Jim, as we read in the diary Tony gave his to Christine, Christine loved the Beatles and music and songs in general, she could still have that one. As for Ben's, I doubt very much if that still exists. Ben would have left it aside somewhere and forgotten about it. Unless he too gave it to someone, anyway, Christine, what's your opinion of her?"

"First impressions, for what they're worth, I think she's a nice girl and she likes Tony, she proved that by helping him to get the job. I can't detect any romantic leanings towards him, romance, marriage and children are not on her agenda. I have no doubt she's one of these women who wants to achieve something and be successful. I suppose she was what is known today as a *career woman,* she's happy enough to be his friend. Writing poetry and songs, and preparing paraphernalia for her rallies seem to be her only interest. And that question mark on her face when he said he'd walk her home, I wonder was that her first inclination that Tony wanted more than friendship."

"I think Jim that she knew from the beginning that he

was in love with her, and that question mark was her first realisation that friendship would not be enough for Tony; that it would have to be all or nothing."

"Then Ted, let us continue with the diaries and see what happens."

"I think we'll take a break Jim, it's a lovely day out, and it's a pity to waste it, I'm getting stiff sitting here.
"You're right Ted a walk to the cove, and a swim is what's needed right now.
"You go for your walk and swim, I think I'll get out the lawn mower and loosen up that way, the forecast for tomorrow is rain; all it will be fit for is reading these diaries. If it's wet early in the morning I'll drive down for you in the car."
"No need to Ted I'll borrow an umbrella from Paul and walk up, see you tomorrow then."

Helen was preparing the dinner when I got there.
"Do you still think you'll get a story?" She asked
"Early days yet Helen, but I'm optimistic, what time is dinner? I was thinking of going for a swim."
"It should be ready around half five."
"I'll borrow Paul's bike."
"Don't be late now; I'm going to bingo tonight."
"Not to worry Helen, I'll be on time."

The cove was quiet, about twenty people scattered along the beach. I swam for about twenty minutes and asked myself, do the people who live along the Copper Coast realise how lucky they are, paradise on their door step. I got dressed and was back in plenty of time for dinner.

At dinner I gave Paul a rundown on what was in the diaries.

He said, "You're still hoping to get something for your paper."

"I am, I can't understand Christine though, I have no doubt she's interested in Tony, yet she wants to keep him at arm's length."

Helen said, "She's young, lots of things going through her mind. She's probably not sure what she really wants, love, career, marriage; give her a chance she'll get there."

"But how long will it take Helen, no doubt love and marriage is not on her agenda at the moment, it's her career only, will she sacrifice everything else for that career."

"Maybe she will, but will she consider it a sacrifice, maybe putting her career aside for love, would to her, be a greater sacrifice."

"I suppose it could Helen, you know I never thought of it like that."

Chapter Fourteen

 The weathermen had got the forecast right, at ten thirty I was knocking on Ted's door just as the rain started to fall.

"Come in, it's a great day for a bit of time travelling, let's delve into these diaries and see what they will reveal."

"Ted I want to ask you something."

"Ask away."

"From the time Tony first met Christine and up to the time he left London, did they remain friends, when Tony realised that all he ever would be was her friend, did they part company?"

"As far as I can remember they remained friends until the day they parted, he quit his job in the book shop a few weeks before that. I think they had a falling out about something, and they didn't meet for a while. I think that's when he realised he was on a road to nowhere. Up to then he never accepted that all they ever would be was friends. He always hoped that some way, somehow Christine would fall in love with him. Think back to the poem Jim, the part where they walked over the heath, and *sat on a park bench in Highgate and talked all through the night.* That was the finale, the

end; over and done with, all hope gone. I think that's
when he told Christine he was leaving."
"So we can only hope Ted that somewhere in these
diaries Tony might reveal what they talked about that
night."
Ted taking his specs from his pocked said, "We can
hope; so let us consult the diaries and revisit the sixties
again."

It was on a Thursday evening; I walked into the
Winchester at around nine o'clock, a quiet little pub off
Avenue Road, it was unusual for me to go out on
Thursday night. I was usually resting and preparing for
the weekend, but Ben had left word at a few of my
watering holes that he would be in the Winchester on
Thursday night and he wanted to talk to me. I had just
ordered a light and bitter when he joined me at the
counter.
He said, "Word has it that you are on a train to Siberia
as far as love is concerned."
I answered, "Early days yet, what are you having?"
"A Light and bitter, no, on second thoughts, I'll have a
gin and bitter lemon."
I ordered the drink and asked, "What's so important
that it couldn't wait till tomorrow night."
"Tomorrow night will be too late; you and I are going to

a party tomorrow night."

"Going to party? Whose party? And where is it?"

"The party is in the gymnasium in the swimming pool across from the library, and it's for a fellow country man of yours, a man by the name of Paddy O' Conner. First Labour Mayor of the London Borough of Camden and also first Irish mayor, he had his inauguration during the week, and tomorrow night he is throwing a party for all those who contributed to his campaign and helped him get elected."

"And you contributed to his campaign? That's why you got an invitation."

"No, I did not contribute to his campaign, and I didn't get and invitation, but that's not going to stop us from going. I have a bet on with the life guards in the swimming pool that you and I will be there."

"I don't know Ben; if it is my kind of thing, why should I bother?"

"Four reasons mate, one, help me win my bet with the security men, two, free drinks for the night, three, support a fellow country man, and four the most important one of all; you need to get a certain woman out of your mind and get back to the happy go lucky fellow you used to be."

"Listen Ben, I have no need to get her out of my mind. I work with her, so we see each other most days, we're friends, and anyway I like having her on my mind, and I happen to like the song, *gentle on my mind*, I'll go to the party with you, for three of the four reasons, now tell me how are we going to gate crash it?"

"I'm friends with one of lifeguards that work there. They have two swimming pools and in winter they board over the one across from the gym and use it for badminton and other games. That's where the food and speeches are going to be, and then it's everyone across to the gym for drinks. There's an exit leading to the loading bay between the gym and the pool, my friend will open that exit at nine o clock and we can slip in and mingle with the crowd."

"Okay so you've solved the problem of getting in, but remaining in there is going to be a bigger problem. I'm sure security will be on the lookout for us, and when they see us we are going to be thrown out."
"We have to remain inside for an hour and a half for me to win the bet."
"So! What are we going to do, become invisible?"
"Don't be a pessimist Tony, once we're in as Micawber would say, *something will turn up*. We'll meet here at eight thirty, have a pint, and then our hands are in the lap of the Gods."

"I thought you didn't believe in the Gods."

"We all believe when we want something."

At eight o clock on Friday Ben and I were in the public bar of the Winchester having a quick pint before the party.

"Do you like my *whistle and flute* mate?" He asked

"Do I like what?"

"My *whistle and flute*, suit."

"Yeah, it's nice, you certainly look the part."

"You scrub up well yourself."

"You know what they say Ben, *It's easy to shine a diamond.*"

"Yeah sure, come on, drink up, we better go."

At ten to nine we were standing in the dark close to the door of the loading bay when it opened, a woman peeped out and whispered, "Are you there?"

Ben answered, "We're here Susan, and thanks."

"Never mind the thanks, get in here quick before someone see's you, you can thank me later."

"It will be my pleasure" Ben said.

The speeches were coming to an end; some of the crowd were already crossing to the gym. And we joined them and entered the gym, where chairs and tables were laid out, a vase of flowers and a little green white and gold flag were on each table, bunting in the same colour vied for seniority with Guinness and Harp bunting. The dinner wine and other drinks that people had consumed were starting to take effect and the noise levels were rising. The smell of expensive scent mingled with the smell of smoke and alcohol. Across from us the strains of an accordion as a three piece band started to warm up. We stood there for a few seconds getting our bearings.

Ben said, "Blimey mate with all the green, white and gold, I think instead of crossing from one room to another, we've crossed the Irish Sea."
"I see they have two bars, one at each end of the room."
"What do you mean Tony?"
"There's a bar at each end."
A barman picking up glasses said, "The one at the far end is Guinness and Harp only."
"Let's go get some Guinness" I said.
Ben answered, "No we'll get a drink at this one first, the middle of the room is still quite empty, and if we march across we will surely be seen."

"You're right, let's have one here first, now what are you having?"
Ben said, "I'll get them" He called for two pints of lager and asked the barman "Have you got the right time

please."

He answered, "It's ten past nine."

"I seem to have forgotten my watch, could you please tell me when it's ten thirty I have to phone the town hall."

"I will sir."

"What's that all about?" I asked.

"I want to establish with a witness the time we got here, and how long we stayed just in case we're thrown out, remember an hour and a half or there abouts will do us to win the bet."

Ben and I stayed at the bar; only about half the crowd had come in from the other room. Of those who had come in quite a number of them were wearing mayoral chains.

I said, "I guess he has invited a few Mayors from his neighbouring boroughs to his shindig." I stood there looking around taking in the lay of the room; it was getting more crowded and noisy as more guests entered.

A very high wall to our left had various climbing equipment attached to it. The top half of the wall to our right had glass panelling with a viewing gallery and a corridor leading to and from the pool. Looking up I could see some members of the public were observing the proceedings in the gym, I also could see two of the security guards scanning the crowd in the gym; I drew this to the attention of Ben.

He said, "I can see them and I can tell you right now, they've seen us, one of them has just pointed his finger and given me the thumbs up."

"I better get us a couple of drinks before we are thrown out."

"A good idea Tony, make mine a double gin and bitter lemon."

The barman was busy; it took him a while to take my order. As I stood waiting to be served someone tapped me on the shoulder. I turned around expecting to see the security men, but to my surprise, standing in front of me was the smiling face of a woman. She was wearing what I assumed was a Mayoral chain over a navy blue jacket and knee length skirt, a white lace top and high heeled black shoes. I put her age at somewhere between thirty and forty, good looking, with brown shoulder length hair.

She said, in a refined English accent, "Excuse me I'm sorry to intrude, but would you mind ordering a drink for me, it's almost impossible to get to the bar."

I was so relieved it wasn't security I was speechless for a few seconds.

Ben said, "Tony did you hear her worship the Mayor?"

"Yes, yes of course, what can I get you?"
"I'd love a gin and tonic."
"Your wish is my command". When the barman came
with our drinks, I said, "A gin and tonic for the Mayor",
and was served immediately.
Ben and the Mayor had found some space a bit back
from the bar, where I joined them and handed her the
drink.
"Thank you ever so much."
"Cheers" I answered.

She asked, "Do I detect an Irish accent, are you friends
of Mayor O'Conner?"
"No, no, just a friend of a friend, my name is Tony
Powell."
"I'm Rebecca Ramsey."
Delighted to meet you and this is my friend Ben
Mason."
Ben said, "Glad to meet you, I think we have a bit of a
problem, do we call you, your worship, your ladyship,
or..."
She interrupted Ben. "Nothing stuffy like that, tonight is
an informal night, but because of protocol I had to wear
my chain of office. Rebecca will do just fine."
The two security men were standing about a few yards
to our left, waiting for the Mayor to move on, and then

pounce on us. As long as we were in her company they would not embarrass her by causing a fracas.

Ben asked her, "Are you acquainted with our new Mayor, Mr O' Conner."
"We meet occasionally, at functions and political events."
I said, "As he is making history by becoming the first Labour Mayor of the Borough of Camden, and he being Irish as well, it would be lovely to meet him."
"My dear fellow, that should not be a problem, follow me."
We marched down the centre of the hall in a line, her worship the Mayor first; followed by me, then Ben, and the two security men bringing up the rear; with a look of amazement on their face.

The bar at this end was more crowded than the one we had left; I could see several Guinness and Harp taps and about six barmen operating them. A large crowd was milling around Mayor O' Conner, but Rebecca's chain of office worked wonders, people stepped aside to let us through. Mayor O' Conner shook Rebecca's hand and kissed her on the cheek and said."Thanks for coming." Rebecca answered, "How could I stay away from such a historic occasion? I'd like you to meet a fellow country man of yours and a recent friend of mine, this is Tony

Powell."

"Delighted to meet you Mr Mayor", I said.

"Forget the Mr Mayor part, Paddy will do just fine."

Then Rebecca said, "This is his friend Ben Mason, not Irish, a Londoner."

Ben said,"Blimey mate I never thought I'd shake hands with a Mayor."

Mayor O' Conner answered, "And why not? As a Londoner I'm sure you have voted for quite a few."

Then he asked me, "What part of Ireland are you from?"

"Waterford" I answered.

Ah *The Déise,* a beautiful scenic county, mountains, valleys, rivers and the wonderful Copper Coast. Ireland's undiscovered treasure."

As he was about to speak to Ben, a fellow Mayor tapped him on the shoulder and gestured for him to go and meet someone.

He said, "Excuse me, but I have to meet some other people. Rebecca will arrange for us to get together some time and compare notes on our respective counties. But for the rest of this night, help yourselves to the Guinness and Harp; or whatever else you want to drink, and Rebecca, if anyone says anything to these two lads, let me know immediately."

Ben handed his empty glass to one of the security men who was standing close enough to have heard the

Mayor, gave him the thumbs up and said, "Will you take it to the counter please," and asked Rebecca and me, "What's your poison?"

Rebecca looked at me.

"He means what's our drink?"

"Gosh, would you believe I've never had a Guinness. I think this would be the ideal time to have my first one."

We mingled and chatted with other people around the hall, some Irish, some English and various other nationalities. When the band started up I had a hilarious time with Rebecca and Ben trying to teach them a half set. Rebecca thought the swing part of the set was wonderful; but said, "For God's sake don't let go or I could be the first Mayor to go into orbit."

Then the band slowed things down with a rendition of *Please release me* Rebecca and I clung to each other as we waltzed around the room; and then up tempo again with Chubby Checker's *let's twist again* Rebecca making a gallant effort to get down in her tight skirt.

At around two o' clock Rebecca said, "I have to go, I have an official function at twelve tomorrow. I told Albert my chauffer to pick me up at two, he's just arrived. "Can we drop you and Ben anywhere?"

Ben said, "I'll stay for another while, I have promised a certain deputy Mayoress a dance."

I said "I'll make my own way home Rebecca."
"Nonsense Tony, you're coming with me, first to my place for coffee, and then Albert will drop you home."
"Who am I to argue with a Lady Mayor?"

Walking to where the Mayoral car was parked, Rebecca and I helped to keep each other perpendicular, and with the chauffer holding the door of the Bentley opened, we fell in, more so than climbed in.
A slight drizzle was falling that glowed orange in the street lights as the chauffer drove carefully towards Rebecca's house. On reaching there he again opened the door of the car and helped Rebecca out. I had to negotiate my own way out and found it a lot harder than getting in.

Rebecca rummaged in her hand bag for her door key and on finding it, said to the chauffer, "Would you mind?"
He answered, "Not at all Mam," and walked towards the door, opened it and stood there as Rebecca stepped inside. She said, "Mr Powell is coming in for coffee, as we may be some time it would be unfair to keep you waiting I will call a taxi for Mr Powell later. Would you please call for me at twelve tomorrow? Good night Albert, and thank you."
"Good night Mam."

Needless to say I never got the coffee; Rebecca took my hand and led me straight to the bedroom, where she kissed me and started to take off my clothes. As she was undressing me, so as not to be outdone, I started to undress her, first her chain of office, which I hung carefully on the bed post, we eventually succeeded in our attempt to relieve each other of our clothes and lay down on the bed.

She said, "Wait a minute, I must have some music," and went to her selection of LP's and choose a Dean Martin one and placed it on the record player, she came back to the bed took her chain of office, reached out her hands for me and said, "I want to dance."
She wrapped the chain around both of us, and to the strains of *Amoré* we danced around the room and eventually back to the bed and collapsed on to it.
She said, "Now prove to me that Lonnie Donegan was right when he sang" *Nobody Loves like an Irishman*.
As my lips touched hers, I mumbled, "You will never again doubt his word"

∧

I said, "Ted...Ted, stop! Stop, hold it... hold it right there. I know you said some things would be farfetched and maybe unrealistic, but this is ridiculous. Are you telling me that the Mayor of some London Borough brought

Tony Powell, a man from... from, next door to nowhere, back to her house in her chauffer driven car, and made love to him?"

"I am Jim and it's true, and I don't think there's anything farfetched about it; you must remember she didn't know who Tony was, or where he came from, she judged him on what she saw and heard that night. He was at the same party as she was, I'm sure she assumed he was invited. Tony when he wanted to could mix with and bamboozle the best of them, as he used to say, *If you can't dazzle them with science, then baffle them with bullshit*, and anyway, you will find more snobbery here than in a city like London, where you are mostly taken at face value, race or creed seldom come into it, you should know that, you live there."

I protested, "But, but, what about Christine?"
"What about her?"
"He was supposed to be in love with her."
"He was in love with her, having sex with another girl didn't change that. When Rebecca and Tony spent the night together, love didn't come into it; it was just sex, and no strings attached. Tony and Rebecca were young healthy people with needs, and anyway if they weren't supposed to do what they did; why were they given the equipment to do it with?"
I got up and looked out the window, a strong south

132

west wind was blowing sheets of rain across the valley, and the trees leaning towards the north east indicated that this was the dominant wind direction here.

I went back to the table and sat down again. I said, "It seems women were attracted to Tony Powell, but why not Christine? She worked with him, she was friends with him, and yet she more or less treated him as a brother, was it because he was Irish? Or because Christine was Methodist, and Tony a Catholic?"
"I don't know Jim it could be a combination of many things, remember Christine was only seventeen or eighteen, a fledging with a dream of becoming a writer. The phrase *sex drugs and* rock *'n roll* was probably first coined in the sixties, you could add a fourth to that, drink! Tony and his mates all drank seven nights a week and sometimes during the day.
Money was plentiful and they never thought of saving for a rainy day. I guess people like Tony saw too many rainy days in Ireland, and I don't mean weather wise, so when they got hold of a few bob they just, as they say *let it all hang out*. Christine didn't drink at all, they were no drink culture in her family, using that old cliché *chalk and cheese*, well those two were definitely *chalk and cheese*. She was a practicing Methodist who taught Sunday school, a musician and poet, Tony was a lukewarm Catholic.

"You mean he was one of those *who sowed his wild oats on Saturday night and prayed for a failed crop on Sunday morning.*

"Tony wouldn't be that hypocritical; he would more likely be nourishing a hangover. I don't know Jim why Christine only felt friendship for Tony, maybe she felt more but never showed it; maybe she was in love and didn't know it; maybe as Paul suggested, she was a closet lesbian. Society was a lot harder on the gay community back then than it is now. But as far as I know friends only they remained, if they did get it together before they left London, he certainly told no one."

"What about the night they walked over the heath; do you think anything happened that night?"

"I don't know; I doubt it, I think you could call that, a walking away walk, two people deciding to go their separate ways."

"God it's all so frustrating Ted, not knowing who she is or where she is, maybe I've read some of her books and I don't even know it, if only Tony Powell had sent you the name that she now writes under we might be able to find something out, anyway we'll continue tomorrow, I got to go."

"You can't go out in that, you'll be soaked, I'll put the kettle on, and we'll have a mug of tea, I have plenty of rashers and sausages, I'll put them on the pan, fry them

with a few eggs, and we'll have a very unhealthy breakfast in the middle of the day, what do you say?"
"You know Ted that sounds a lot better than walking home in the rain."
"Without a doubt and as it looks like the rain is here for the day, after eating we'll delve back into the diaries and see is there any progress in the love lives of Christine and Tony."

Ted had lit his fire early, even though it was wet and miserable outside it was lovely and warm in the kitchen, it didn't take him long to cook the late breakfast, or early dinner, call it what you like and we sat there eating and talking.
"What are the Irish doing now in London Jim? Are they mixing more, integrating more, becoming involved. Back in the fifties and sixties all they wanted to do was to create a replica, or a mini version of what they left behind. They had no interest in becoming involved in the culture of that country.
The people Tony and I hung about with were mostly English, they were our friends and we did what they did, we became involved and lived the way they lived. London is like a huge roundabout and different cultures from all over the world circulate there, and I think it a shame that people don't mix and learn. What's the point of someone like me, from a country back ground

trying to re-create that in one of the biggest cities in the world?, That's what creates a ghetto, people afraid to mix, to reach out, to become involved."

"I don't know Ted, some people like to keep their own culture, and pass it on."
"I agree with you, I'm not saying that people should forget their own culture, what I'm saying is they shouldn't be afraid to embrace new ones. When I was in London I could have put on a Waterford jersey and gone to New Eltham on Sunday morning and watched Gaelic football, but I might as well have stayed here in Waterford and gone into Walsh Park."

"So! What did you do"?
"I didn't go to London to spend the week down a drain digging, and come up at the weekend and go to an Irish dance. I went to visit several Museums, I went to see many shows in the west end, to the London palladium to see some of the top acts of that era, I went to Stamford Bridge to see all of the top soccer teams, I went to Villa Park to a cup semi final, to Wembley to a final, I went to Lords to see a cricket match, to Twickenham and to Wimbledon, I spent weekends in Brighton, Southend-on-sea and Hastings."
"Yes, we know what you were doing in Hastings."

"What I'm trying to say Jim is, I wanted to observe, to learn, to educate myself. I hope the people who are emigrating today, whatever part of the world they are going to, that they will try and integrate with the culture of that country. They don't have to abandon their own culture, but not shove it down the throat of their host country. Now that's the end of today's lecture, let's finish this meal and throw these dishes in the sink and get back to the diaries and the *swinging sixties* and learn some more about Christine and Tony"

Chapter Fifteen

It was on a Thursday evening, I was sitting in a quiet
corner of the Winchester enjoying a pint and browsing
through a book that I had picked up in the book shop.
Then Ben walked in and said,
"I was hoping you would be here, I have some good
news."
I asked, "What are you having?"
"Nothing thanks, I'm working, I'm on a quick break, but I
just had to tell you, we are going to Wembley on
Saturday to see Chelsea and Spurs in the cup final, a
London Derby."

"You're joking; pull the other leg, it's impossible to get
tickets, they're like gold."
"I know, but I'm telling you I have two."
"How may I ask did you manage to get hold of them, are
they legit, are they forgeries?"
"Hells bells Tony what do you take me for, as if I'd be
party to something illegal, they're legit, straight up."
"Well then how did you manage to get them?"
"I think I might have time for a quick pint, get one in and
I'll tell you."

I got the pint; brought it to the table and said, "Now tell me how you got hold of these tickets."

Ben took a mouthful from his pint, rubbed his mouth and said, "I was working as a bouncer at a night club down west last night. This guy I know, Basil Gordon he's a regular there, he's got a boutique on the King's Road; so naturally he's a Chelsea supporter, this girl Sharon was sitting at a table on her own, waiting for her man, Psycho Sid."
"Christ Ben you mean to tell me there are women out there willing to hang out with someone who's called Psycho Sid."

"A free lunch Tony and a good time, Sid is never short of a few bob, he runs several businesses, and all shady, if it was straight Sid didn't want to know.
He had an aversion to anything straight. He was pulled up once by the old bill for suspicion of drunk driving, he refused to walk a straight line; said it was against his principles, and I can tell you he was a real Psycho. He didn't get his name from taking in stray kittens, and he'd as soon kick your teeth out than shake hands. Anyway Sharon and Basil are having a good chat and a laugh when in walks Sid, he sees Basil chatting to Sharon. He goes right over to their table; lifts Basil up by his King's Road lapels gives him a right bollicking and

was about to head butt him when I stepped between them.

I shouted, "Sid, Sid, hang on, calm down, it's not what you think."

He said, "Piss off Ben, or you'll get what he's going to get."

"Hang on a minute mate; I'm to blame for this."

"I didn't see you chatting up Sharon, this toe rag was. "

"I know Sid but I asked him to do so, let me explain. Sharon was sitting here on her own waiting for you, some of the other punters were pestering her and I asked my mate Basil if he would do me a favour and keep her company until you came."

Sid shouted, "Sharon! Is that true?"

"Sure Sid, that's it, that's exactly what happened."

Sid let go of Basil's lapels, and said, "Get out of my sight you ponce" and pushed him across the floor, and sat down beside Sharon, shouted at a waiter and ordered a bottle of champagne.

Basil said, "A god job you interfered when you did Ben, I owe you one."

"All in a nights work" I answered.

"I'll say one thing for you Ben you do meet some colourful people, but the tickets what about the tickets?"

"Basil lived to enjoy the rest of the evening and when he was leaving with a good looking piece of form on his arm, he said thanks mate and he pushed something into my top pocked. I thought it was a tip, but when I pulled it out, I couldn't believe what I had, and it was two stand tickets for Wembley. And to top the evening off when Sid was leaving he dropped me a pony; "for looking after Sharon" he said.

"I'll be a monkey's uncle, talk about the devil looking after his own, two cup final tickets and a twenty five pound tip, if you fell into a sewer Ben, you'd come up tasting of chocolate."
It's the finishing school I went go Tony.
"Yeah I know the streets of London and then the army."
"Don't knock it unless you've tried it. Now are you available on Saturday? Or are you off with Christine to a demo to torment L B J again?"
"No, no demo, I'm available. I wouldn't miss it for the world."

"How are things with you and Christine?"
"Much the same, still friends, getting on great, we talk, joke, laugh, discuss the world and its happenings, but nothing of a passionate nature. Christine shows great passion in her poetry and songs, but it seems it is impossible for her to transfer that passion from the

written page."

"Maybe she hasn't met the person she wants to transfer it to yet."

"I suppose I must accept that could be the case."

"Must be frustrating for you mate, maybe some night next week we'll sojourn down west, and with a bit of luck meet someone who will relieve some of that frustration, anyway I must be off; see you in here early on Saturday."

At one o' clock on Saturday afternoon Ben and I, along with several hundred people were walking up Wembley way, the banter was good among the opposing supporters, mostly good humoured, and odd insult thrown in here and there.

"What are our chances?" I asked Ben.

"I'm worried Tony, Peter Osgood is a big loss, our leading scorer out with a broken leg, but I guess that's the way the cookie crumbles."

The atmosphere in the stadium was electric, the band struck up, playing several popular tunes, the conductor up on a make shift podium, the fans sang along with the band, a rapturous roar when they played *blue is the colour* likewise when the Tottenham song was played, time seemed to fly, all the ceremonies finished; and the game kicked off.

We cheered and roared our way through the afternoon, tried to convert every chance. I nearly kicked Ben in the shin when I lashed out at an imaginary ball, threw our hands in the air in frustration at ever missed chance, and though the ref was bald as an egg, we shouted at him to take the hair out of his eyes. Deep dismay when Jimmy Robertson scored for Spurs and Frank Saul added to our woes when he put Spurs two up. Our hopes rose when Bobby Tambling pulled one back with five minutes to go, but alas it was not to be. The ref blew the final whistle, and with that whistle went our hope for glory. We were left to rue the absence of Peter Osgood. The Chelsea fans filed out of the stadium, most of the Tottenham fans remained inside to cheer on their heroes.

Ben and I went into a pub called the Royal Oak, to let the crowd disperse, and then back to the Swiss Cottage to drown our sorrows, and boy did we drown them. When your Karma is in the wrong direction and the Gods ordain that it's not your day; there is only one thing you should do. Stay in bed and pull the bedclothes tight around you, turn your face to the wall and your backside to the world and pretend you're a little furry animal in hibernation waiting for the warm sunshine of spring.

There must be millions of paving slabs in the City of London, and that night at around one o' clock while trying to walk home the toe of my shoe found one of those slabs that was about a half inch above the rest. If it was the only one in London that was above the rest, I have no doubt that on that particular day my toe was going to find it. Over I went, my forehead striking the footpath; there I lay dazed and spread-eagled on the ground. After some minutes I slowly picked myself up and managed to negotiate my way home without any further mishap and fell into bed.

A noise woke me. I lay there in my bed, my eyes closed, trying to figure what the noise was; it's the roar of the ocean I said. I struggled to open my mouth; my tongue would make sandpaper feel like porcelain. To say my head ached would be an understatement, it felt like at least six pneumatic drills were mining for nuggets of wisdom in my head. Someone's voice told them to pack it in, that all they would find there was sawdust, how could anyone even with an ounce of wisdom wake up in this state. It took a few minutes for me to realise that the voice was mine.

I opened one eye, then the other, looked around the room, eventually realised where I was, in the middle of London, and the noise was the roar of traffic, not the ocean. My mind tried to put together the jigsaw that was yesterday, starting from the morning, it worked its way piece by piece; from the Winchester to Wembley, to the Royal Oak, and back to the Swiss Cottage. I slowly crawled out of bed and made my way to the toilet, then looked in the mirror, my God I said what happened to you? Both sides of my face were caked in dry blood. It was then that my brain clicked in the last piece of the jigsaw, my collision with the pavement. I turned on the tap and washed the blood from my face to reveal a deep gash right through the centre of my left eyebrow, that was the only cut I had, it seems while twisting and turning during the night the blood ran down both sides of my face.

I made myself some black coffee, when I had it finished, I decided to go to Chalk Farm to the Pembroke Arms where some of us meet most Sunday mornings for a quiet drink and consume some of the free cheese and crackers that were always on the counter. As I approached the Pembroke I could see Christine and two other girls walking towards me. I knew they were coming from a nearby Sunday school. As I didn't want Christine to see the condition I was in, I waved my hand at her from a distance and crossed to the other side of the street. My two legs went like putty, whether it was the loss of blood, the effect of yesterdays drink or the appearance of Christine; or all three, I don't know. I barely made it to the Pembroke and quickly sought out a bar stool.

Ben asked,"What happened to you? You look like something the cat brought in; come to think of it no self-respecting cat would bring in anything that looked remotely like you."
"Get me a pint quick Ben."
"Did you have a fight with some Tottenham fans after we parted?"
"No, no, nothing like that, I tripped, I bloody well tripped over a paving slab."
"That's a nasty gash you have there, it will need stitching. You should get yourself up to Hampstead General."
"Maybe later Ben, right now I need this pint and maybe one or two more with it, Christ we drank too much yesterday crazy, bloody crazy."
"I know Tony, but it's not every day your club get to Wembley. Listen I seriously think you should go to the Hospital, my mate Bill will be picking me up soon, he won't mind driving you there."
"I suppose you're right, I'll go with you when you're going."

Ben's mate Bill dropped me on Hampstead High St; from there I walked to the hospital and into casualty, I was still feeling under the weather, so I leant against the wall for support.

A nurse asked, "Are you all right?" and on seeing the cut over my eye, said, "No you're not, come with me."

I followed her into a small room.

She said "Wait here, I'll go and find a doctor."

The room had a wash hand basin, some storage cabinets, and a high bench type bed in the middle of the floor covered with rubber sheeting.

The nurse came back.

Taking some swabs from a drawer she said, "Let's have a look at that eye. Nasty, and it's not fresh, makes it harder to stitch. Were you part of the cup final trouble yesterday?"

"No, I tripped over a paving slab." And then the doctor entered.

"What have we here? Left over's from yesterday", he said.

The nurse answered, "No doctor, he tripped over a paving slab."

The doctor said, "I see, and what's your name."

The doctor was an Asian man of about forty, "Tony Powell," I answered.

"Tony I'm going to have to stitch that, but first an injection to make things a bit easier for you, please lie here on this bed, good, now just relax."

He gave me an injection in the forehead; just above the cut and as everyone know you won't find much flesh on that part of your anatomy. Christ did I feel that injection; the sweat came out through me, or was it alcohol? I thought I was going to faint. I felt every stitch he made; I thought he'd never end, but at last he did.

He said, "There, finished the nurse will put a band aid on there, and then you can go. You better give him some pain killers."

I said "Thanks."

"Try and look where you're walking, and don't go head butting the pavement again," he said as he left the room.

The nurse put a band aid over the stitches, gave me a glass of water and the pain killers, "You can go now."

I got off the bed, and got a bit of a wobble.

The nurse said, "I'd advise you to go straight home to bed; you've lost a lot of blood, do you want me to call a taxi?"

"I'll be fine, and thanks."

"You're welcome, good bye now."

I walked back to Hampstead High St, I still felt as if I was going to faint, I barely made it across the street. I had to sit on a street bench for some minutes to get my strength back. I saw a telephone kiosk close to me and decided to phone Christine. The phone rang a few times and then Christine answered.

Christine it's me, Tony. I just want to tell you I won't be able to work tomorrow; I had a bit of an accident."

"What happened?"

"I had to get some stitches over my eye."

"Were you fighting after the match?"

"No Christine, I wasn't fighting, I fell; will you be okay tomorrow? I don't think I can make it in the morning, and I'm working in Fleet St tomorrow night. I can be in the book shop at one on Tuesday."

"That will do fine; dad is here all day tomorrow and on Tuesday morning, so two o' clock Tuesday will be grand; by the way, why did you go to the other side of the street to avoid me this morning?"

I needed to sit down again so I answered, "I'll tell you Tuesday; right now I need to hail a taxi and get myself home to bed, bye for now." I went back to sit on the bench, the cold sweat again poured out through me, after about ten minutes I felt better. I walked to the edge of the footpath and hailed a taxi to take me home. When I got there I went straight to bed and didn't get up until five o'clock on Monday evening.

I made something to eat and then got the bus to Fleet St, managed somehow to get through my shift, and when it finished I went home and back to bed again. Got up at twelve, washed and shaved, walked to Finchley Rd and had something to eat.

 I walked into the bookshop at one forty five. I was hoping Christine would have forgotten about Sunday morning by now, or at least have put it to the back of her mind.

First she said, "Give me a look at your eye," and then asked, "Are you sure you weren't fighting? I read in the papers about some trouble between Chelsea and Tottenham supporters."

"Christine for the umpteen times, I wasn't fighting, I tripped over a paving stone."

 "Okay, now tell me, why did you avoid me on Sunday morning? And don't say you didn't, it was obvious."

"I hadn't been to the hospital, and the cut on my eye was still exposed; and I was feeling weak from the loss of blood, I thought I was going to faint, I didn't want you to see me in that condition."

"If I had known you were in that condition I would have made sure you went straight to the hospital, not to the pub."

I wanted to tell her that I wasn't too sure whether it was

the loss of blood or the sudden appearance of her on the street that made me feel the way I did, but thought better of it.

^

Ted left the diary on the table. "I think we'll take a break Jim, what do you think now?"

"I think Tony Powell is developing a bit of a drink problem, and to think he's in love with a girl who never takes a drink, she spends her Sunday mornings teaching Sunday school while he is being put back together in hospital."

"That's a bit harsh Jim, that was just a once off; Wembley, the cup final, a long day. I don't think we had a drink problem, if we had we didn't see it as a problem, it was our way of life."

"The fact that you are here talking to me now Ted, seems to make me forget that you were part of it all."

"I was, and I drank my pints then and I'm still drinking them today, maybe not as much, and it hasn't done me any harm. The drink culture has changed Jim, we might have met seven nights a week, but all we drank was three or four pints."

"That's a lot of drink in a week Ted."

"Maybe it is, maybe it's not. When we went to the pub it was for a chat, debate, discussion; company, call it what you like. The young people today only go out the weekend, and their intention is to drink as much as they can, as quickly as they can; and dispense with reality and enter a state of oblivion. All sorts of mixtures and concoctions, their weekend is not deemed a success unless they end up vomiting and collapsing in someone's door way.

If you did that in our day you were seen as someone who couldn't hold their drink and was to be avoided.

Maybe Tony was drinking a bit too much before he left London, but I think the fact that he was getting nowhere with Christine made him seek the pub and company more often. I have no doubt that if Christine felt the way about him as he did about her, he would have spent all his time with her."

"I just can't understand Ted why she was willing to be such friends with him and nothing more."

I don't know Jim, maybe it was the drink, maybe it was; I don't know, it could have been many reasons, maybe there's a simple natural reason for it."

And tell me, what would that be?"

"Just because a man falls in love with a woman, doesn't mean that she will automatically return that love. People fall in love every day of the week, fall in love with someone they have no business falling in love with.

Fall in love with someone's wife, with someone's husband, women fall in love with women; men fall in love with men. Love causes as much heartbreak as happiness. I think we really have no say whatsoever when it comes to falling in love, it just happens and we have no control over it, who can explain it? I would call it a complicated enigma."

"An enigma is bad enough Ted, but a complicated one really compounds the issue."

I got up and looked out the window, the rain had stopped. I said, "The evening is brightening up, I better be going, Helen will have the dinner ready."

"I'll drive you."

"No need to, I'll walk, I need to stretch my legs, I'll call sometime tomorrow and we'll continue with the diaries."

"Are you going for a pint tonight?"

"I don't think so Ted, I hardly ever drink on week nights."

"Neither do I much, but the weather has confined us indoors all day, I just thought it would be nice to get out for a while."

"Okay, I'll meet you at around half nine."

At dinner I asked Paul if he would come for a pint with us.

"No Jim, I'm going to the pictures in Waterford."

"Are you going on your own?"

"No, I'm going with my girlfriend."

"I didn't know you had a girlfriend."

Helen answered, "He met her two weeks ago, but I have no doubt she won't last long; they never do."

"Maybe this time Helen, this could be the one."

Paul said, "Will the two of you give it a break? How are the diaries going, have you discovered what pen name Christine is writing under?"

I updated Paul on our progress, and added, "All we have discovered, I think, is that Tony Powel had a drink problem, whether he overcame it or not has not yet been revealed."

"Do you still think you can get a story out of it?"

"I hope so, but whether that story will be good enough for publication is another matter, but if I get something for the paper that will do."

"If you get a story you could send it to an agent."

"I know Paul, but these days it's harder to get an agent than a publisher."

"Helen said, "Write it first, and then worry about publishing."

"Paul said, "I must get myself ready, can't keep a girl

waiting."

Helen said, "Why don't you ask her to dinner next Sunday?"

"It's a bit early for that mother."

"I'll help you with the dishes Helen."

"Not at all Jim, you get yourself off to meet Ted, do you want a lift?"

"No thanks, the evening has turned out grand; I need a bit of exercise after that feed."

I had a shower and shave and then walked to the village.

The pub was busy when I walked in, some locals and a lot of holiday makers all enjoying the wonderful scenery along the Copper Coast. The remnants of the daytime fire gave out a little heat. I ordered a pint of Guinness, before the barman had it pulled Ted entered. "What are you having?" I asked.

"I'll have a bottle of Guinness please Jim."

The barman asked Ted to throw a few blocks of wood on the fire, saying "The evening is a bit chilly."

We brought our drinks to a table a bit away from the counter.

Ted said, "It's nice and cosy here, and it's one of the few remaining pubs in the country that doesn't have a dual personality."

"What do you mean?"

"I mean Jim that this pub is a pub, and it's not masquerading as a restaurant, God how I long for the old days, the smell of a pub not a restaurant, stale beer and cigarette smoke. You know at Christmas time I often see the video of Shane McGowan's *fairy tale of New York*, Shane sitting at the piano, his drink on top of it, a cigarette in an ash tray, a bluish haze of smoke wafting up towards the ceiling. That's the way pubs used to be, and should still be, it's no wonder most of them are empty now, you walk in at night, and what greets you? The smell of bacon and cabbage or fish, God almighty it's enough to turn your stomach."

"That's the way it is now and I think it's for the better, at least your clothes won't stink with the smell of smoke, and it'd good for the health, Ireland is changing Ted, old ways slowly going, I think as far as the pubs are concerned it's adapt or close, I think it would be grand to go to a pub at night, sit on a high stool order a coffee and talk to your friends and drive home."

"Ah well, I suppose you're right but it's hard to get the old ways out of your system, what you were reared with seems to stay with you. In our day change came so slow; what we had, we had for years. These days things change every week, you hardly have a chance to get used to something when it's been replaced. You buy some commodity this week and next week it's obsolete, but I guess that's the way it is now. When you left this evening Jim I was thinking of what you said about Tony, and a drink problem."

"Why Ted, have you changed your mind? Do you think he had a drink problem?"
"I know for sure up to the time he met Christine, he hadn't, but as I said before, from the time he met her, his life completely changed. He wanted to be with her all the time, time away from her was time wasted. I flicked through a piece of the diary after you leaving and I chanced upon one excerpt, and reading it, well you would have to agree that he had a problem; because if he wasn't with her he was in the pub. And when it became obvious to him that all she wanted was friendship he spent more and more time in the pub and though the pub never interfered with his work; the last year he spent in London, it was from work to pub, to bed; and to work and the pub again."

"You would have to wonder why a man like Tony Powell would leave London. After all London was where it was all happening, he was young; he was at the centre of things. He had all the time in the world, you would think that he could achieve what he wanted to achieve; and he leaves it all and moves to Australia, what's the saying, something like, *if you're tired* of *London, you're tired of the world."*

"I've told you before I have no idea why he left Jim, maybe a combination of things. I have no doubt Christine was part of it, perhaps the drink, maybe he realised he couldn't keep doing what he was doing; so he just left, I'm hoping somewhere in the diaries he might explain it."
"It's hard to believe that Tony never went back to London; you'd think he would have got in touch."
Why Jim? He made his decision. Christine was happy with friendship, Tony wanted love, which was never going to happen so he burned his bridges, walked away and kept walking."
"They're both getting old now, do you think before they depart this world that they will eventually meet, if only to say goodbye again."

"I don't know; I just don't know; maybe, maybe not, anyway let's have another drink."
"Why not, I'm on holiday, you're retired; we have no work in the morning."
"We're not the only ones who have no work in the morning, since the country collapsed most of the people are on the dole, or have emigrated, nothing here for them only misery, and to think the people who caused

this devastation are walking around free with big pensions. W B Yeats said, *that's no country for old men,* now it's no country for poor men, or middle income men, it's a country run by the rich, for the rich. I'll get that drink."

Ted came back with the drink.

"Cheers, to the future."

"To the future Jim, if we have one, will you call around in the morning?"

"I will if you don't mind, I hope we can get to the end of the diaries before I go back to England."

"I don't mind, I like reminiscing about those times, I suppose you could say it's uniting me with old friends again. Is Helen calling for you?"

"Not unless I phone her, but it's such a bright night I thought we'd walk."

A man went out the door and seconds later came back in with a guitar.

"Looks like we are going to have a session," Ted said.

Most of the visitors sang and then called on the locals. I said, "My friend Ted here sings a good song, come on Ted give them, *Over the Heath.*

"No not tonight Jim, but seeing that most of you are visitors here to our lovely Copper Coast, I'll give you a recitation I saw in the local paper in praise of this area; it's called,

The Copper Coast."

The Copper Coast; what is it? Can you give me an answer? It's a work in progress; it's a young and old dancer.

Millions of years in the making, it is yesterday and today, it's also tomorrow and our D N A.

It's a song of the sea, a lament on the wire and crafted by ice, water and fire.

It is poetry and prose, and it is art and it's craft; today being serious, tomorrow just acting daft.

Now it is farming and factories where once it was mines; it's eating and Guinness, it is red and white wines.

It has got lakes and walks inland and on shore; caverns and taverns and a welcome at the door.

It is a fisherman on the rocks, a boat out on the blue; it's swimming and diving and kayaking too.

Its mackerel and lobster, seals here and whales; and wave skipping speedboats and wind in your sails.

It's calm and in turmoil, a beauty; a beast and a razor sharp wind blowing up from the east.

It's a roaring sou' wester, forming huge land battering waves, and thunderous noises emitted from caves.

It is a sea safety centre to organise searches, it is Dilisk and winkles and sea birds on high perches.

It is castle and cottage, grassland and bog; damp swirling mist and dense drifting fog.

*It is a beautiful evening in the middle of June and waves
on the beach rehearsing a tune.*

*It has been a home to paupers and kings on the throne,
and the sound of the fishing boats as they make their
way home.*

*It's a picnic, a bar b q; a walk hand in hand, building
sandcastles and your shoes full of sand.*

*It's a walk on the wild side and wish you were here, or a
snooze in the evening on your favourite chair.*

*Mountains and rivers and valleys so green, it's a home
for the young and old and all in between.*

*It is sunbathing and lazing and doing nothing taxing, it's
just hanging out and your surfboard need waxing.*

*The Copper Coast, what is it? Well it's sadness and
laughter; it's your father and mother; your son and your
daughter.*

*It's the here and the now and the long, long ago, it is
summers warm sunshine and winters cold snow.*

*It is what it is, a never ending refrain, can you spare me
a few hours and I'll try to explain.*

*So let's fill up our glass and all drink a toast, to the best
scenery in Ireland, the famed Copper Coast*

Ted got a great cheer from both locals and visitors alike.
I said, "That was brilliant Ted, if I was anywhere in the
world and I heard that being recited, all I would have to
do is close my eyes and I would be right here on the

Copper Coast; wonderful."

"Thanks Jim, now let's have one for the road and then we'll be off."

Chapter Sixteen

After yesterdays wind and rain today is a complete
contrast, a lovely summer's morning, Ireland no doubt
has a diverse climate. After breakfast I went for a swim
at the cove, nobody else had arrived yet. It was like
having my own private beach, the water was crystal
clear, and standing jaw deep I could clearly see my toes.
I swam out to the mouth of the cove, lingered for a
while then swam back in, dried myself and walked to
Ted's. It was around eleven o clock; Ted was sitting in
the garden reading his paper.

"I see you've been to the village already Ted."
"No I haven't, my good neighbour Biddy brought me the
paper."
"I went for a swim; it's like paradise over there, the
beach deserted, it's like being the last man in the
world."
"Do want a drink, tea or coffee?"
"I'll have a coffee please."
"You stay here I'll make the coffee and get the diary; it's
such a lovely day we'll read it out here."
I sat there waiting for Ted, hearing nothing only the
sound of nature; I was reminded of a couple of lines of a

poem I had read somewhere.

Season of colourful flowers and happy hearts, dancing singing and seaside play / birds and bees and other summer sounds form a choir to sing you through the day.

Just as Ted came with the coffee and diary a young couple, about nineteen or twenty passed on bicycles on their way to the sea.

He said,"Ah how I envy them, to be that age again, if only for one day, for one glorious summer day, to be young and care free again. To be in love, to be in Tramore on a summer's evening having fun on the bumpers and hurdy gurdys, to listen to Brendan Boyer on the juke box singing *Kiss me Quick*, to eat chips from a vinegar soaked brown bag.

To walk from the Atlantic Ballroom on to the beach with the one of your dreams, and admire a full moon casting a shimmering silver streak of light on the surface of the sea. To experience once more what it's like to be in love, and to be loved, to walk her home and kiss good night, and then spend a restless night in joyful anticipation of another day. No need to die to go to heaven, what could be more heavenly than a summer's day with the one you love?

Young girl in summer dress / her lovely face the sun caress.
Nimble of limb she walks by / I watch her pass, I heave a sigh,
recalling days that used to be / alas those days no more for me.

Days of youth, days of bliss / days of love and tender kiss.
Those teenage years so full of joy / and first love for girl and boy.
Nights of love dance and song / those carefree days are now all gone.

Gone, gone... gone forever, memories where would we be without them?" Ted handed me the coffee and diary.
"Is that poem a lament for the past Ted?"
It's for the past and the present. The first line in John Keats poem *Endymion* is, *a thing of beauty is a joy forever.*"
"And so it should be Ted."
"It should be, but it's not".
"What do you mean? Surly you can enjoy any form of beauty you like, when you like."

"You would think so, but I'm only allowed to enjoy certain forms of beauty. Young and old can gaze upon, and admire the beauty of a sunset or sunrise, young and old can gaze upon, and admire a beautiful sunlit grove of bluebells, or the golden sheen of furze on a hillside, young and old can admire a beautiful work of art., or an old or new piece architecture. But if a young lady walks by, only the young are allowed to gaze. If an old man admires her beauty, he is deemed a pervert. The world does not seem to understand that the ability to appreciate all forms of beauty does not deteriorate with old age. Now let's delve into these diaries once more and see if Tony's appreciation of Christine's beauty is anyway diminished."

It had been one of those wonderful hot summer days in London, so hot that at times it was uncomfortable and even now at eight in the evening it was still warm. I was sitting outside the Swiss Cottage enjoying a cool ale shandy and observing the world go by. I heard a voice saying,
"I was hoping I'd find you here."
It was Christine.
"What brings you this way? Can I get you something to drink?"
"If you don't mind I'll have a coco cola with some ice."
I went to the bar got the drink and brought it back to the bench and asked, "What can I do for you?"

Can you come in at ten in the morning, I know you're
not due to start until two, but dad is going to
Birmingham to a book fair on the eleven o clock train
from Euston and he wants me to go with him,
something about me getting to know people in the
trade, if I'm going to eventually take over from him.
We're staying overnight, back about eleven on
Thursday."
"No problem with that Christine, I'll be there at ten; and
I can do Thursday morning as well."
No need to do Thursday, just put a notice in the
window, *Opened at eleven thirty tomorrow,*
dad will open then."

"Are you going to take over from your father?""I don't
know whether I'll take over from him or not, I know
that's what he wants, but I can't see myself in that book
shop for the rest of my life. I'd like to pursue my own
career, doing what I like doing best, writing, composing;
but can I be successful at that. Is it just a foolish
dream?"
"A dream, ambition call it what you like Christine. I
suppose you could say that's what gets us out of the
bed in the morning. If we accept that every day of our
life is going to be a repeat that would make life very
hum-drum. We have to have something to aspire to,
even if we know we are in pursuit of the unachievable;

we still have to try and achieve it, and that's what keeps us going, that voice somewhere in the mind that say today is the day."

"So you believe Tony that, trying to achieve something is as good as achieving it."

"No I'm not saying that Christine, but the hope that we can achieve it keeps us going."

"Maybe you're right. Don't you think it's time you took that plaster off your eye?"

"I've been trying to, but it seems to be stuck to the hairs of my eyebrow."

"Let's have a look."

"Take it easy now, nice and gentle."

Christine rubbed her finger across the plaster, and then one quick pull, and it was off.

Ouch! I shouted. "Why did you do that?"

"That's the only way to do it, no dillying or dallying about it."

"Well fancy meeting you here, can I get you a drink?"

It was Ben and the girl from the swimming pool who had let us into Paddy O Conner's bash.

"No thanks I'm fine, this is Christine, you met her in Chelsea after the Man U match, remember?"

They both shook hands, and Ben introduced Susan.

I asked, "What bring you this way on a Tuesday

evening?"

We're meeting Jill and Steve, I don't think you've met them; they work with me in the Library, we're going down west for a meal. Would you care to join us?"

I looked at Christine, she shook her head.

"No thanks we've both got an early start in the morning, thanks all the same but we'll skip this time."

A Hillman Imp pulled in close to the pavement and the hooter sounded, a woman whom I assumed was Jill shouted at Ben to, "Get a move on."

"That's Jill and Steve, we better be off, see you the weekend."

"Enjoy your meal; see you when I see you."

Christine said, "I better go, can I get you a drink?"

"No thanks I'm going myself, I'll walk with you some of the way."

The traffic was very heavy, so I caught Christine's hand as we ran across Avenue road; we walked to the book shop that way, hand in hand.

At her front door she said, "See you in the morning before we leave."

We stood facing each other; a voice inside me said it's now or never, and I kissed her.

Walking home I was in ecstasy, I even sang a verse of *on the street where you live.* I couldn't believe I had actually kissed her, and I said, "It is indeed a wonderful world."

Trade was brisk all day Wednesday in the shop; a young woman came to the counter with a copy of J P Dunleavy's *The Ginger Man*.
"Have you read it?" She asked.
"Yes I have, I can highly recommend it, a wonderful read."
"What's it about?"
"It's about the antics of a wayward student at Trinity College."
"I'll take it."
I put the book in a bag and said, "Anything else."
"I don't know you have so many books here, I can't make up my mind... could you recommend one."
"I've just finished reading Thomas Hardy's *Far From the Madding Crowd* it's a great story."
"I never heard of him."
"You don't know what you're missing, I guarantee when you read it you will come back for more of his books, and I can recommend Walter Macken's, *Brown Lord* of *the Mountain*."
"I think I'll take Hardy's one."
I went and got the book from the shelf and said, "Enjoy."

The afternoon passed quickly and soon it was time to lock up. I walked down the road with pep in my step. I went into a small little cafe of Finchley road; I ordered steak and chips with a fried egg and apple tart for dessert. I had just started to eat when Ben walked in. Sliding on to a chair, he said, "Great minds think alike" and added, "That looks good, I think I'll have the same, a repeat of that" he said to the waitress pointing at my plate.

"How did it go last night?"
"Good! We had a great meal and went on to a club; I've had no appetite all day, until now. Did you and Christine stay long in the Swiss Cottage?"
"No we left just after you, I walked her home, and then home myself for an early night."
"Do I detect that you are a bit more upbeat than what you have been of late; that cloud of doom and gloom that's been hovering over you seems to have blown away, has your walk home with Christine last evening anything to do with it."
"Yes I am in a good mood, and yes it has to do with Christine I think things are going to work out."
"Why do you think that?"
"I walked her home last night, and on the way we held hands and when we reached her house we kissed."
"What kind of kiss?"

"What kind of a question is that? We kissed, as in lips coming together."

The waitress came with Ben's food, he thanked her. "What I'm asking you Tony is this, did she kiss you or did you kiss her?"
"We kissed each other, I kissed her and she kissed me."
"Are you sure she kissed you? Did she put her two arms around you? Did she prolong the kiss? Did she kiss you a second time? Did she hold you tight afterwards?"
"No she didn't prolong the kiss and no, she didn't kiss me a second time, she just said good night; where are you going with this Ben?"
"I'm just trying to establish if ye kissed each other, or you just kissed her."
"Christ Ben what's the difference?"

"There's a big difference in kissing and being kissed, I don't want you to get your hopes up and then be knocked down again."
"God I'm sorry I mentioned it at all, let's change the subject."
"Did you see her today"?
I said, "Let's change the subject. And no, I didn't see her today; she's gone to Birmingham with her father. She's coming back tomorrow, and I'll see her then. Are you going for a pint?"

"No I'll have an early night, I'm banjaxed after last night, what about you?"

"I was going to have an early night also, but now I'll think I'll go for a couple of pints."

"Well enjoy them."

"Don't worry I will, I'll see you the weekend."

When I left the cafe I walked towards the Winchester, then changed my mind, turned around and walked home, I had been in a good mood all day, but Ben's lecture on kissing and being kissed left me feeling down. When I got home I plugged in the kettle and made myself some tea, sitting at the table drinking it Ben's words came back to me.

I had kissed Christine, but had she kissed me? Ben and his *holding me tight, and did she prolong the kissing* what difference did that make? No she didn't put her arms around me or make any attempt to prolong the kiss, and when it was over she just stood back, looked at me, and said good night and went indoors. Maybe Ben was right, I had kissed Christine but she hadn't kissed me. I turned on the radio, got undressed and went to bed and I fell asleep listening to Joe Cocker singing *I'll get by with a little help from my friends."*

I didn't waken until after ten, got out of bed and had a bath, and then made a mug of coffee; I didn't feel like a breakfast so when I finished my coffee I went for a walk towards the Heath. It was a good sunny day, a lot of people on the Heath, mostly mothers and children, some nannies minding other people's children and a few joggers. I sat on a park bench; Christine and Ben were still on my mind. Had she kissed me or not, or was Ben right, it was just a one way kiss and I was reading too much into it. The fresh air had given me an appetite I decided to walk back to the Railway bar for dinner. The lunchtime crowd hadn't come in yet so it wasn't too busy, I ordered a pint of bitter and asked for the menu, the menu and pint came together. I ordered gammon, egg and chips; it would serve as breakfast and dinner. I took my pint to a table and waited for my meal.

I entered the book shop at two o clock Christine's father was serving a customer.

"Is Christine here?" I asked.

"In the print room" he answered.

Christine's back was turned to me. She was leaning over the print machine.

"How was Birmingham?" She didn't answer; I thought she can't hear me with the noise of the machine I went around to the other side of the machine.

Christine looked at me, she was crying.

I asked, "What's wrong? What happened?" I went to hold her, but she pulled back.

She said, "Sorry you must think me silly."

"I don't, but why are you upset?"

"You, me, and us" she answered.

"Why? What did I do to make you cry?"

"You kissed me."

"I'm sorry Christine, if that upset you."

"No, no, I'm not upset because you kissed me; I'm upset because I didn't kiss you back, and I know you wanted me to, but I wouldn't, I couldn't. I know how you feel about me, but I can't return that feeling, I can't let feelings get in the way of my plans. I'd love to love you, but I can't, maybe I don't know what love is, would I know if I was in love. I must pursue my career that's my first priority, love and all the baggage that goes with it would only be a hindrance."

"Christine, it's all right, don't cry."

"It's not all right, you love me, and I'm afraid if I don't love you, we'll go our separate ways, and I don't want that, I want us to stay together, remain friends but for you, that's not enough."

She ran from the print room and climbed the stairs two steps at a time.

Her father was still inside the counter, the customer he was serving had left, and the shop was empty.

"I don't understand, I didn't mean to upset her."

He answered, "Christine is complicated, always has been, her dreams are not the dreams of the average girl of her age, love, a husband, a house and family. She's a poet, a songwriter and she wants to be an author, she can't fall in love with you, or with anyone else for that matter, she can't let that happen, she won't let it happen, it would only get in the way of her goal in life. So she had to make a choice. It seems she's made that choice; and that choice is her career above everything else.

I know how you feel about her Tony, but you have to accept the choice she's made. Now you have a choice to make. Do you want to remain working here in close proximity with her every day, knowing that all you'll ever be is her friend, can you accept that? Will friendship be enough for you?"
"I don't know I need time to think."
"Yes, think about it and also think about this. Christine's decision now is her career, she says she hasn't time for love, is that because she has never fallen in love, if... say tomorrow, or the day after she meets someone and falls head over heels in love with them; will she still put her career first? So Tony if you decide to stay here hoping someday she may fall in love, she may fall in love all right, but there's no guarantee it's going to be with you."

"I know that, but that's a chance I'm willing to take."

"You're young Tony, Christine is young, and you both got your whole life ahead of you, don't ruin that life by dwelling on something that might never be, accept it and move on."

"That's easier said than done."

"The shop's not too busy, I'll manage on my own, and it's a nice day out, why don't you take the rest of the evening off, go for a walk on the heath, observe and enjoy the world."

I closed the bookshop door behind me, stood on the pavement for a while deciding which way to go, to the heath as Christine's father had suggested, to the Swiss Cottage, home or the cinema? No contest, the way I was feeling the Swiss Cottage won hands down.

I called for a whiskey and a pint of Guinness.

The barman said, "Scotch?"

"No, I'll have a Jameson." I took my pint and whiskey to a table in a quiet corner of the pub, to mull over in my mind what Christine and her father had said.

I had no doubt now that all Christine wanted was friendship, even though she knew I loved her, should I stay around in the off chance she might someday fall in love with me, or could what her father said happen. She might fall in love with someone else, and if she did, could I accept that, could I still work with her, still meet her everyday and act as if everything was all right. I didn't think I could, decisions would have to be made.

When the barman came to collect some empty glasses, I ordered another pint; he returned with the pint put it on the table and handed me my money back, saying, "That lady at the counter paid for that."
Ben's friend Susan was coming over.
"How are you?" She asked.
"I'm good, are you meeting Ben here?"
"No I Just popped in for a quick coffee, just to get away from the smell of chlorine for a while, I've got a swimming class at five, and you're starting on the pints early."

"I guess it's been one of those days; it was either a walk on the heath, the cinema, home or the pub, the pub won."
"There's a picture on at Odeon across the way, *Midnight Cowboy,* Dustin Hoffman and John Voight are in it, it's good, Ben and I saw it last week, you should go see it."
"Maybe next week, not tonight; are you and Ben? I mean..."
"We're just friends, an odd night out, the cinema or a meal, and whatever goes, no strings attached."
"And you don't mind if he sees someone else, or he don't mind if you see someone."

"Of course we don't mind. We're not married or anything like that, it's all just a bit of fun, enjoy life while you can."

"I suppose you're right, no point in taking life or women serious. Will Ben be in later?"
"I don't know he might be I think he's got a door job tonight, he might pop in for one beforehand. Remember Tony there's more than one fish in the sea and all of them have the same thing on offer."
"Has Ben been telling you things?"
"He just said that you were besotted by Christine, and for her it's strictly friends."
"I know there's more than one fish in the sea Susan, but it is the one we can't catch, that we want the most."
"I know Tony; it's always been like that, forbidden fruit and so forth. I must be going, take care, and go easy on the drink."
The pub was getting busy, the night customers were coming in, and I went to the toilet, got another pint on my way back and went back to the table.

A voice behind me said. "I see you're on Hari-kari Boulevard early tonight."
It was Ben. "What are you on about?" I asked.
"Drink, he answered; you seemed to be determined to leave behind the Monarchy of England for the Republic

of oblivion."

"I'm just having a few drinks, nothing to worry about."

"What happened? You were in a good mood the last time I met you, has this anything to do with Christine?"

"I hate to admit it, but you were right."

"What was I right about?"

"About me kissing Christine, and did she, or did she not kiss me. She told me today, strictly friendship, nothing else."

"I don't think you hitting the bottle will solve anything; you're not going to find her love at the bottom of an empty glass, all you'll find there is emptiness, drink never solved anything."

"Christ Ben, who are you to talk about drink, you take a drink."

"I know I do, a social drink, company, conversation, debate, you won't find me sitting alone in a bar trying to drink myself into oblivion. That's not going to solve anything, that's not going to impress Christine."

"I'm not trying to impress anyone; all I'm doing is sitting here enjoying a quiet drink in peace, so please let me get on with it."

"All right Tony, if that's what you want, but whatever chance you have with Christine when sober you have no chance at all when drunk, she being a tee toteler and a bible basher to boot."

"She is not a bible basher, for God's sake, she helps out at Sunday School that's all, and she never mentions religion, even when I was interviewed for the job, either her or her father never mentioned religion, it never came into it. Whatever she thinks of me, religion has nothing to do with it, she is a nice quiet kind persons and also a lady, no she is more than a lady, a lady would feel inferior in her presence, now if you are not having a drink then get out of here and let me enjoy mine."

"God you are obsessed with her, talk about putting someone on a pedestal, but I have an offer you can't refuse, and get your mind of Christine at the same time."

"My mind is not on Christine."

"Yeah right; don't bother getting up I'll get the drinks, a pint of Guinness is it?"

"Are you sure you don't mind buying me one, won't that make you a party to me joining the Republic of oblivion."

"Very funny, I'll get the drinks first, and then all shall be explained."

Ben said, "Cheers" handing me my pint.

"Slainte," I said.

"What in God's name does that mean?"

"Health Ben, it means health, now tell me, what's the offer I can't refuse?"

"I have a date this weekend, and I want you to come with me."

"Do you want a chaperone?"

"No I don't, let me explain, I have a date with Sandy, Sandy Jacobs, you haven't met her, she often comes in to the Library, and she lives in Golders Green."

"Oh! I see a piece of posh tosh, and you want me to be there when she gets undressed, to pick her clothes of the floor fold them neat and tidy and hang them in the wardrobe."

"No nothing like that, if you give me a chance I'll explain, her parents are away for the weekend and her friend Jane is staying with her. Sandy has invited me around on Saturday night and I want you to come with me, to make it a foursome."

"Oh! I get it now; you want me to distract Jane while you have your way with Sandy."

"No, I'm offering you a chance to have a good time, go for a meal, a few drinks, then back to Sandy's, listen to a bit of music, a dance or two, and maybe, just maybe get your mind of Christine, it's up to you. If you don't want to come, I'll find someone else."

"You said her name was Jane, what's her second name, any chance she's a plain Jane?"

"No, she's not a plain Jane. Her name is Jane Babington; she's a good looker, black shoulder length hair with a turn up at the end, a bit like Elisabeth Taylor.

"Sure, and I'm Richard Burton, okay I'll go with you, it should be a bit of fun, and as your friend Susan said, there's more than one fish in the sea, what time do you intend to go."

"Susan was here?"

"Yes she came in for a coffee, just to get away from the chlorine."

"Meet me in here on Saturday evening; I told Sandy we'd be there around six, oh and bring something to drink with you, a bottle of wine, whatever you can get. Now I got to go I'm working down west, if you were a bit sober you could have come with me."

"I am sober, are you having one before you go?"

"No thanks, I must be going, see you Saturday evening."

When Ben left I went to the bar for a pint and a half one, and had several more before the barman decided I had enough.

He said, "Sorry Tony that's it, no more, I'd hate to see anything happen to you, do you want me to call a taxi?"

"No, no, no, no, I'm fine, just, just one more and I'll be off."

And then I fell over a bar stool.

The barman said, "That's it I'm calling a taxi."

Ten minutes later he was loading me into the taxi, gave the driver my address, and took some money from my pocket, and said, "You should have enough in that. He'll be sorry in the morning."

I staggered from the taxi to the front door, after several attempts I finally got the key in the lock, managed to get to my room and fell on to the bed. I lay there until my mouth started to dry up, then I remembered the bottle of sherry I had won in the darts raffle at the Winchester. I found the sherry at the bottom of the cupboard, opened it and lay back on the bed.

I can't remember drinking it, but as I lay there my body seemed to leave the bed and float up towards the ceiling and there was two of me in the room, one lying on the bed, the other levitating in mid air looking down on the one in the bed.
All I remember after that, is vomiting into the toilet, I made my way back to the bed and lay there shivering and trying to figure out what happened. Had I died for a few seconds and started to leave this world or was it all a dream, but it seemed so real. I could see the two of me so clear, one stretched on the bed, the other up against the ceiling

The next thing I remember was hearing a phone ringing somewhere in the house. I struggled to open my eyes, the top of my mouth was stuck to the bottom, I raised my hand, eventually my watch came into view, ten thirty it said, a voice in my head asked is that today or tomorrow. I crept out of bed and tried standing and found I could manage it. I got up, washed and shaved, made myself some coffee and feeling sick sore and sorry I walked to the bookshop.

I asked her father, "Is Christine here.
He pointed towards the print room door, "Go through".
A ray of sunlight was shining through a skylight; Christine was standing in it looking at a poster she had just printed. Richard Harris was singing *MacArthur Park* on the radio. The sun gave her hair a golden glow and her face was as white and as smooth as ivory, I wanted to reach out and hold her there and then, she looked so beautiful even Michelangelo would have gazed at her in awe.

"Good morning" I said.
She turned around; "My God she said you look like death warmed up, what happened?"
"I'll be alright don't worry it's all self inflicted."
"I'm sorry about yesterday Tony, the tears I mean, and all that silly talk about love and making such a fuss over a kiss, I was being a bit dramatic. I hope it won't affect our friendship; we're still friends aren't we?"
"Of course Christine, yes... friends, you and I friends forever."

"Good, now let's put yesterday out of our minds, can I get you a cup of tea, coffee?"

"No thanks, I'm okay."

"I think you need to get a hobby Tony, keep you out of the pub. I know it's hard to stay indoors on your own all evening, but surely you can find somewhere to go besides the pub. Why not go to night classes, or join an amateur dramatic society, do something with your time besides drinking."

"You could be right; I'll see; maybe night classes would be good."

Mac Arthur Park ended abruptly and a voice said, *we are* sorry *to interrupt this programme but we have an important news flash. The civil rights leader and peace activist Martin* Luther *King was shot dead in Memphis Tennessee last night.*

Christine dropped the poster she was holding. "No... No, why? Why? My God, my God, why shoot a man of peace?"

I went to her, put my arms around her and she wept the tears of the compassionate on my shoulder. The ray of sunlight shone on the words on the poster that fell to the floor. *Make, love, not war.* As I held her I thought she wants to pretend that yesterday never happened, and things to be as they were, but is that possible?

Ted took off his glasses, took a hanky from his pocket, wiped his eye, blew his nose, and sat there looking into space.

"Are you alright?" I asked.

"I'm fine, fine, it's, the diaries, memories, all coming back, Christine, Ben, me."

"And Tony," I said.

"Yes, yes, of course; Tony."

"What the hell happened to him in his room, floating to the ceiling and all that; do you think he had an out of body experience Ted?"

"More like an out an out of mind experience. I have no doubt at that time in his life he had a drink problem, if he wasn't with Christine he was in the pub."

"And Christine and the kiss and the tears...Do you think she really thought that Tony could pretend nothing had happened."

"I don't know Jim, I suppose Tony had brought things to the fore by kissing her, up to then she could pretend that Tony was happy to be just friends, but that kiss changed things. Tony was in love with her; would he be content to carry on just as friends? Even though she didn't love him, she was drawn to him in some way that she didn't understand, and she hoped her rejection of his love wouldn't drive him away."

We were interrupted by a knock on the door, Ted dropped the diary and went to the door, and it was Helen.
"Is Jim here?" She asked.
Yes he is come in, Jim it's your aunt."
Helen said, "Jim the day is so good I'm going to show you some of our beautiful county; I thought a trip up to the Comeraghs, visit the magic road and the Mahon falls, and then on to Dungarvan for dinner."
I answered," Sounds good, I've heard of the Mahon falls, but what's this magic road?"
Ted answered, "It's a road up the mountain where if you stop your car at a certain spot and turn off the engine, and release the handbrake you get the impression that the car is going up the hill from its own accord.
"That's interesting defying the law of gravity; I'd like to see that."
Helen said, "Ted here has a good recitation about it. If you ask him nice he might recite it."
"Come on Ted, let's hear it."
"No, Jim I only recite when I have a few pints in me."
I asked Helen, "What about Paul, will you have to get his dinner?"

"It was Paul's idea, he phoned me and said to take you out and about and that he's going around to the girlfriend for dinner."

Well then that's settled, a tour of the county it is then."

Helen asked Ted if he would like to go with us.

"No thanks Helen, I've been sitting reading most of the morning, I could do with a long walk. But you can't go right now, Jim hasn't eaten since breakfast, and I'm sure it will be after four before you have dinner, so Jim you put the kettle on and I'll go to the garden for some scallions, lettuce and radishes. I'll chop and mix them all and I have some Kilmeaden cheddar in the fridge that should sustain you until you get dinner."

"I do feel a bit peckish, that sounds great."

"Right, you put the kettle on and I'll get the vegetables."

"I'll call back in an hour" Helen said.

Half an hour later we had finished our tea and were ready to go.

"I might go for a pint later Ted, will you come?"

"And you think Tony Powell had a drink problem."

"I'm on my holidays, what's a holiday without a few drinks."

"As I'm on a permanent holiday I may as well join you."

At nine thirty Ted was walking to the village. The pub was very quiet when he entered; just two elderly people

whom he knew were at the counter. He said, "Hello
Paddy, hello Mick, not many about tonight."

Mick answered. "Since austerity has kicked in the young
and middle age has disappeared from the pub, the only
people who can afford to drink now are those of us who
are old enough to have a pension and their mortgage
paid."

Paddy said, "I wonder if the Government and the E U
are aware of the damage that austerity is inflicting on
the people, and if they are, why are they continuing
with it?"

Ted said, "I think our politicians haven't a clue, they just
make it up as they go along; no wonder people have lost
all faith in them, "And then called for a large bottle of
Guinness, and was just about to pay for it when I walked
in.

"How was your tour of the County?" Ted asked.

"Great, it was very scenic."

"You must be thirsty, gallivanting around the
countryside all day, what are you drinking?"

"I'll try a pint of Guinness, you know what really amazed
me was the magic road, defying the law of gravity, when
Helen turned off the engine and released the
handbrake, you'd swear to God the car was
freewheeling up the hill."

"I have a copy of that poem about the magic road;

remind me to give it to you before you go back, and by the way when are you going back?"

"I'm going on Sunday, we should be finished the diaries by then."

"We should, another session or two should see us through."

"I wonder Ted will we ever find out what name Christine is writing under, I'd love to get her book and read it."

"We can only hope that we will, let's finish the diaries and see what happens, do you want to continue with them in the morning for an hour or two, and if we do the same on Friday we should be at the end of them."

"Yes, we may as well get on with it. We have to see it through now, maybe all shall be revealed in the end, now let's have another couple of drinks and then we'll walk home."

I was up early, and after breakfast asked Helen if I could borrow her car.

"Of course you can Jim, all you have to do is ask and you can have it anytime."

"Thanks Helen, I think I'll drive the Copper Coast to Tramore and take in some of the sights."

I drove to Bonmahon to visit the Geopark centre; a beautiful restored old Church of Ireland Church. On display there the geological history of the Copper Coast and the copper mining heritage of this area, books of local interest can also be purchased there, and refreshments. I drove the wonderful scenic route along the coast, stopping to take a photo of the abandoned old mine building and its chimney stack, past The Art Hand studio and on to the rugged cove of Kilmurrin. The sun was shimmering on the sea as I stopped the car in the top car park.

I got out my camera and took a photo of the Sculpture that told the story of the origins of the copper coast. A white sailing boat with red and white sails glided past. I took a few snaps of the boat and then drove down to Boatstrand, walked down to the dock and took some photos of the boats. From there on to the remains of Dunhill Castle; this stood on a promontory above the winding road and the river Anne, a reminder of Cromwell's invasion of Ireland and its turbulent past. I climbed the steep steps to the Castle to its highest point and took some photos of the Anne Valley Walk. Then back to the car and on to Fenor and a walk through an ancient bog. My next stop Tramore.

I bought a container of coffee and walked the mile long sandy beach, walked back and sat on a bench on the prom and observed the sights and sounds of people on holidays enjoying themselves. Screeches of merriment emerged from the amusement park, the smell of fish and chips that drifted on the air made me hungry so I bought a tray of chips and a hotdog. As I walked back to the car, music blared out from various gaming arcades, I sat in the car eating, and observing the people as they passed to and fro all dressed in multi coloured summer clothing. I arrived back at Helen's at about twelve thirty.

"Did you enjoy your morning?" Helen asked.
"I really did, no doubt we have some wonderful scenery here in Waterford, yesterday the Comeragh Mountains, today the Copper Coast."
"That's true Jim. Are you calling to Ted's today?"
"I'm going over now."
"Will you have something to eat before you go?"
"No thanks Helen, I had some chips and a hotdog in Tramore, I'll have a cup of tea at Ted's."
"Okay, be back for your dinner around five."
"I sure will; I wouldn't miss one of your dinners for the world."

Chapter Seventeen

Ted was cutting his lawn when I arrived.

"Sorry Ted I didn't realise you were busy, I'll call back later."

"No it's all right Jim, I'm just finished, I've done enough for today, come on in and I'll make us a pot of tea, would you like a sandwich."

"No thanks, I've already eaten; the tea will do just fine."

A stiff sea breeze had blown up with the turn of the day so we decided to have the tea indoors.

Ted said, "A couple of hours at the diaries today, and maybe tomorrow that should see us through, I'll get them."

He came back with the diaries, poured the tea and said, "Now let's see if Tony is still in pursuit of Christine, or has he given up the chase."

On Saturday evening Ben and I were trying to draw the attention of a taxi in Finchley road, eventually one saw us and pulled into the kerb.

"Golders Green please mate," Ben said.

"Anywhere in particular in Golders Green" the driver asked.

Ben gave him the name and number of the road, and the taxi driver set the meter in motion and edged into the traffic. Each of us had a bottle of wine, I had a red and Ben had a white. At around five thirty we were walking up the garden path to Sandy's house, Ben rang the bell, and a woman with fair hair and a crease in the middle and wearing a blue denim minie skirt and a multi coloured blouse opened the door.

She hugged Ben, "Glad you could come, and she reached her hand out to me, saying "This must be your friend Tony."

"Tony, this is Sandy."

"I'm delighted to meet you".

"Come in; come in", she led us into the sitting room, saying "Jane, Ben and Tony have arrived."

Jane came in, Sandy introduced me, saying, "This is Tony; you've met Ben before."

Ben had been telling the truth, she certainly was no plain Jane, black hair combed to one side, she wore a short sleeved low cut blue dress that ended about three inches above her knee, a glass of red wine in one hand, and she reached her other hand out to me, saying, "Delighted to meet you."

"The pleasure is all mine," I answered.

Sandy said, "Let us go into the parlour."

Ben said, "We've brought a couple of bottles of wine."

"Bring them with you."

We followed Sandy and Jane down the hall and into the parlour, Jane took the wine and placed it with several other bottles on a large drinks cabinet.

"What would you like to drink?" Sandy asked.

Ben answered, "I'll have a gin and bitter lemon."

"And I'll have a whisky and water please."

"You are not a wine drinker then," Jane said.

"Yes sometimes, when I'm having a meal."

Sandy said, "Jane could you put on some music please". Jane selected a forty five, *please release me* by Ingelbert Humperdinck, and placed it on the record player. Sandy brought us the drinks, now she said, "Let's get this weekend started," come on she said to Ben, "Let's dance."

Jane and I sat on the sofa.

"What part of Ireland are you from?" She asked.

"Waterford, have you ever been there?"

"No, I've been to Ireland though, my Grandmother came from Kilkenny, my parents brought me over once, when I was about ten years old. All I can remember of it is cows and countryside, and some young fellow hit me in the ankle, trying to hit a ball with something like a hockey stick."

"It's called a Hurley; in Waterford we call it a Hurley, though in Kilkenny they call it a Hurl."

When the record finished, Sandy put on a Beatles L P, come on you two she said, "Get off your backside and get out here for a dance."

"Do you want to dance?" I asked.

"Let's have another drink first."

The two of us went to the drinks cabinet, poured our drink, took a few sips, and then placed them on the small counter in front of the drinks cabinet.

I asked, doing an exaggerated courtesy.

"May I have the pleasure of this dance kind lady?"

"You certainly can sir," She replied.

The two of us invented some new moves as we danced to *she said she loves you* and when finished collapsed on to the sofa.

Ben said, "A couple of more drinks, and we're out of here."

"Where shall we go?" I asked.

"I hear tell that's there's a real good Indian restaurant on the High Street, dinner there, and then on to the Bull and Bush."

"Sounds good to me" I answered.

Ben had been right about the restaurant; we had a lovely meal there. Jane and I were getting on well, and after the meal we walked hand in hand to the Bull and Bush. And we sang *down at the old bull and bush* in the

Bull and Bush, and what with the drink and Jane, I postponed reality and confined Christine temporally to the back of my mind.

At closing time Ben asked the barman to call a taxi.

We were back at Sandy's at around one o clock. Sandy opened another bottle of wine, put on a Frank Sinatra record, and as "old blue eyes" sang *strangers in the night* Jane and I danced entwined to each other around the floor.

Ben and Sandy were already exploring each others anatomy on the sofa, so Jane and I danced out to the hall and stumbled and fumbled our way up the stairs to Jane's bedroom and on to her bed. I could hear Sinatra singing, *I did it my way,* I answered, "So will I Frank... so will I."

Sunday morning and the sun shone through the window as I looked around the room, trying to get my bearings and wondering where I was. My mouth was dry, and I had a slight head ache, a blackbird sang clearly in someone's garden, as the events of the night before slowly revealed themselves to me, and realising where I was a rather strange thought entered my head. Why does the blackbird here sound the same as the ones at home, shouldn't he be singing with an English accent. Then someone stirred beside me and I remembered Jane, "Good morning" I said.

"Is it?" She asked.

"Well a blackbird is singing its praises."

"What time is it?"

"It's just gone ten o'clock; do you want to use the bathroom?"

"You go; I'll rest here for a while."

I splashed some water on my face, used someone's tooth brush to wash my teeth, when I returned to the bedroom Jane was asleep. I dressed and went downstairs.

Ben said, "Good morning, do you want Coffee?

I answered, "Several cups."

Sandy came in dressed only in her underwear. "I'll have some as well", she said.

Ben handed us the coffee, I sat on the sofa to drink mine, and Sandy went to the window.

She said, "What a beautiful morning", and then, "No, no, God above in heaven, no!"

"What's wrong," I asked.

"It's my parents! They're home, mum has just got out of the car and dad has driven it around the back."

Ben said, "I thought they weren't back until tomorrow."

"So did I, quick you must get out of here."

"Tell us how, and which way?"

She said, "Upstairs, quick upstairs, and when they come in you can climb down the drainpipe."

Ben and I made a run for the stairs, watched out the window as Sandy's dad unloaded the car. When he finished we slid quietly down the drainpipe, climbed over their neighbour's fence, out their path and walked casually down the road.

I said, "That was close, I often heard of people climbing down a drainpipe, but I never thought I'd have to do it." The two of us took a fit of laughing and then walked to the High street to call a taxi.

Just as we reached the High street a police car braked to a halt right beside us. A policeman jumped out and said, "Hold it right there."

"What's wrong?" Ben asked.

Then the driver got out, a woman officer.

She said, "We just want to ask you a few questions, where are you coming from?"

"From a friend's house, just back the road," Ben answered.

"What's the number of the house?"

Ben gave her the number.

The policeman said, "Both of you turn around and put your hands behind your back."

"Why?" I asked.

"Just do it," he said.

He handcuffed both of us, and said, "I'm arresting you both on suspicion of burglary."

The woman officer started to read us our rights.
Ben said "Hang on a minute you're making a mistake, we are not burglars we were just visiting friends."

She asked, "Do you normally leave your friends house through the window. We have had a report of two people who fit your description climbing out a window."
"We can explain that," I said.
"I'm sure you can; you can do it back at the police station, now get into the car."
Ben said, "No, no hang on a minute, this is ridiculous; I can explain everything here and now, no need to go to the station."

I said, "Yes give us a chance, do we look like burglars."
She answered, "You don't have to look like one to be one, come on let's go."
Ben said, "Wait, wait, we were visiting friends, Sandy and Jane, Sandy's parents came home sooner than expected, we had to make a quick exit."
"Why?" She asked.
I answered, "We stayed overnight, and we didn't want to get Sandy into trouble."
"A likely story, "she said.
"It will be easy to prove it" I said
She asked me, "How can you prove it"
"We'll get into the car, you drive back down the road

and Sandy will confirm our story."

"We can't do that," Ben said.

"We have to," I answered.

"If we do that we'll get Sandy into trouble."

The woman officer said, "I'm off duty in twenty minutes, so I happen to be in a good mood, now get into the car I'll drive down to the house."

Ben said, "No, Sandy's parents are very religious, very strict..."

The policeman said, "Obviously Sandy is not, listen let's sort this out once and for all. I'll knock on the door say I'm inquiring about some disturbance in the area last night and if her parents were away as you say, they will call Sandy; I'll bring her down to the car and she can identify you, or not."

Sandy came out to the car with the policeman, identified us and said she was sorry; a neighbour had seen us climb down the drain pipe and called the police; she apologised to the police for wasting their time and thanked them for being discreet.

"That's sorted then," Ben said.

The woman officer answered, "Not yet, we're off duty as soon as we get back to the station, we're not going to have time to write up our report."

"So what happens now," I asked.

"We're going to have to hold you over night and write

the report in the morning."

What? You can't do that, we're innocent; all you need do is forget about it and let us go," Ben said.

She said, "Oh I don't know, you're not that innocent, I can think of a few things I could charge you with, taking advantage of an innocent girl in the absence of her parents, trespassing in someone's garden."

"You wouldn't? Would you?" I asked

"She would you know," the policeman said.

Ben said, "You know we did nothing wrong, you can't lock us up."

She started the car, turned and drove up towards the high street.

I said, "For God's sake take off these cuffs and let us go."

She stopped the car and started to laugh; and said, "You should see the look on your face," she got out, opened the back door and said, "Out, and turn around", she undid the handcuffs, "You're free to go."

"Thanks," I said.

"What's your name," Ben asked?

"Penelope, Penny to my friends."

"Can I call you Penny?

"Maybe, if you stop climbing through young ladies windows," and she waved and drove off.

Ben waved down a taxi, and said, "Swiss Cottage please."

"We had a narrow escape there Ben."
"I know Tony, but she is a good looker."
"Don't tell me you have forgotten Sandy all ready."
"No, no, of course not, but I wouldn't mind taking Penny out."
"It's Penny now is it, a few minutes ago she was going to lock us up for the weekend."
"I think she was only having us on, maybe I'll phone the police station someday next week and ask if she would like to come out for a drink."
"You're joking."
"No, I'll give it a try."
"Well you know what they say Ben, *God loves a Trier*

^

"Well Ted, has all the dust cleared by now."
"What do you mean Jim?"
"I mean since we started reading these diaries, your memories of what happened back then must be clearer."
"Yes they are, I'm glad you heard me sing that song, or poem call it what you like, I'm glad you questioned me about it."
"The song wouldn't have been much good without the

diaries Ted; they are filling us in on what happened back then if all we had was the poem we probably would have to resort to fiction."

"I know, and you didn't want that, lucky they turned up when they did."

"Yes that was a piece of luck, and I think Ted that the poem and diaries were written by two different people."

"What makes you think that?"

"The Poem is all about events, about what Christine was doing and trying to achieve back then, no talk of love or romance, no mention of Tony or how he felt about her, no mention of any name, either pen or real, while the diaries make it very clear about what he felt for her and mentions both their names. If we assume that Tony wrote the diaries, then I wonder who wrote the poem?"

"I have no idea Jim."

"Tell me do you remember the last piece you read, when Tony and Ben got arrested."

Yes I do as I read it; it began to come back to me, I remember Tony telling us about it in the Winchester, and you know the following week Ben phoned the police station and asked for Penny and asked her out."

"Did she go out with him?"

"Yes she did, and if I remember correctly when I left London she was still with him."

"What about Sandy and Jane? Did Tony or Ben ever meet them again?"

"I don't think so, just another one night stand and I have no doubt that Christine had priority in Tony's mind the following day."

"From the time Tony met Christine, apart from one night stands, did he ever have what you might call a steady girlfriend."

"No Jim, no one steady, he took plenty of girls out, a night or two, a week, two weeks the most; and then he went his own way. I think he went to night classes for a while, work, and the pub an odd trip to Stamford Bridge; cinema, theatre, though before he left it was mostly the pub. That was his life until he left London."

"And Christine Ted, nothing ever became of it?"

"Friends, only friends, he still worked in the shop, went on rallies with her, but all strictly as a colleague and workmate, and then one day he left. I remember the night he came into the Swiss Cottage, Ben and a few of us were having a quiet drink. He said he had called to Australia house sometime back and everything was settled and that he was going home to Ireland for a week, and then back to London, and on to Australia. And that was that."

Paul knocked and walked in, "How are the diaries going?" he asked.

I answered, "Good, I'm getting to know a good few of Ted's friends, and the antics they got up to back then."

"And Christine and Tony are you any wiser where they are today?"

"I'm afraid not Paul, nothing yet."

"Ye must be nearly finished them by now."

"A good few pages left, but their whereabouts not revealed yet. It looks like we'll finish the way we started, no idea what name she's writing under, or where she or Tony are."

Paul said, "That's disappointing, all for nothing."

Ted said, "It's disappointing, but it hasn't been all for nothing. Some of the things we got up to back then I'm sure Jim can weave some kind of story out of them."

Paul said, "Dinner is almost ready so we better get a move on; we don't want to incur the wrath of mother on us by missing one of her dinners."

"Are ye going for a pint tonight? Ted asked.

Paul answered, "I'm not, because I've got a date."

"I'll join you Ted, say around nine o' o clock, I'll give you a shout."

"Grand Jim I'll see you then."

At dinner Helen asked, "How are you progressing with the diaries?"

I answered, "Good, almost there."

"Will you get a story from them?"

"I hope so Helen, it would help if I knew where Tony and Christine are now, and what name she's writing under."

"So you haven't come across any clue in the diaries yet."

"No Helen nothing so far and we're almost finished."

Helen said, "It's rather surprising when Tony sent the diaries to Ted that he didn't mention what name she is writing under or at least put his address on the letter. If he expected Ted to put some kind of story together it makes no sense not to send a contact number or an address."

"Maybe he doesn't want to be contacted," Paul said.

"Why send the diaries at all then?" I asked.

Helen said, "All I can say is, he wants a story; but only about the past, about the time he writes about in the diary. If you can get a story out of it, he wants the end of that story to be when he left London and nothing after that. Nothing about the present nothing about where he is now, nothing about where she is, or who she is. He doesn't want the name she writes under revealed; he's trying to keep the then and now well apart."

I said, "But surely he must realise the story won't be complete without finding out where he is today, or if he and Christine ever met again."

Paul added, "And without finding out what name she is writing under."

"I don't think that would be too important, but we have to know if they ever made contact. If this is going to be a love story, we have to know if they lived happily ever after, or that they never again met."

"Aren't you forgetting one thing," Paul Said?

"What's that?"

"The poem, if we go by the poem they must have had some contact, otherwise how would Tony know the name she writes under."

"I'm not forgetting the poem, but you are assuming that Tony wrote the poem and that he knows her pen name. What if someone else wrote the poem, and is it true? We know some of it is true from what we read in the diaries, but what about the part about her becoming an author, is that true? Or is it just the figment of someone's imagination, I must press Ted on it maybe he can throw some light on it."

I walked to the pub enjoying the summer evening and the scenery; a kestrel hovered over a field for some moments and then dived on its prey, an evening meal for the Kestrel, death for its prey.

In the country side you are closer to nature than in the city. You notice the signs and happenings of nature more, a flock of seagulls flying back to the sea after a day's scavenging in some inland dump, a fox slinking along by a distance ditch its head down and tail between its legs, rabbits panic and dash towards their burrow as I approach; cows lying down enjoying the evening sun and contentedly chewing the cud. In the city all you notice is people, buildings and traffic. I suppose you could say the buildings obstruct your view of the city. I left the brightness of the evening sunshine outside and entered into the cool darkness of the pub, and had just ordered a pint when Ted came in.

"I timed that well" He said.

"What are you having?" I asked.

"I'll have a bottle of Guinness please Jim."

The pub was quiet, no shortage of seats at the counter, Ted poured his Guinness, and I waited for my pint to settle.

"Ted, Helen, Paul and I were talking at dinner, about the poem and the diaries. Helen expressed surprise that Tony didn't send his address with the letter, or at least a phone number."

"I suppose he don't want us to know where he is."

"Why Ted? What difference will it make if we know whether he is in New York or London? If he wants a story, we knowing where he is would only help to write that story, we could contact him; ask him if he knows the name Christine is writing under, ask if they have met since he left London. Why send you the diaries at all if he is not willing to cooperate."

"I don't know Jim, I think he wants to keep the past and the present separated, maybe he's not too concerned about a story and just sent them to me for old time's sake."

"I thought the contents of the poem might make a good story, the diaries confirmed it. If I was trying to get a story just from the poem only, if the diaries didn't exist I could understand that we had no hope of cooperation. But the fact that he sent the diaries to you and mentions a story, it doesn't make sense that he wouldn't want to cooperate."

"All we can do Jim is finish the diaries, and hope between the poem and the diaries that you can weave some kind of story, or something to satisfy your editor."

"When did you get the poem Ted, last year, two, three years ago?"

"I'm not sure Jim; why? What difference does it make?"

"If we take the poem as truth, and if Christine is being published under a different name, if Tony wrote that poem, then he knows that name so he must have had contact with her. Or was the poem just sent to him, and like us he has no idea of what name she's writing under, maybe they have met and are together now."

"I don't know if they are together or not, I don' know if they have met, maybe if Christine sent the poem she also sent a letter telling of her change of name and the name of the book."

"I guess that's a possibility, but if he does know her name and the name of the book, why didn't he tell you when he sent the poem. Helen thinks that Tony wants a story but only about what's in the diary, nothing about the present, he doesn't want Christine's name revealed or where he is or even who he is."

"What do you mean, who he is?"

"I mean if Christine changed her name, maybe Tony changed his."

"Why would he change his name?"

"I don't know Ted, maybe if Christine is writing under a different name, and say if she and Tony were at some event, and some paper mentioned Tony's name and whatever name Christine is writing under. Those who knew Tony back then might put two and two together and realise who she really is, I'm just grabbing at straws. But if Tony had a different name, then anyone he hung around with in the sixties seeing that name wouldn't take any notice of it. You said Tony has travelled a lot, Australia, America, we all hear about the illegals and the undocumented maybe he had reason to change his name."

"Listen Jim; let's forget about where Tony and Christine are or what name she writes under, or what name he is using. Whatever name they are using now they are not the Christine and Tony of the sixties, times change, people change. If they have changed their name, then they have changed as well. So let's just concentrate on the diaries, and you write a story about the two main characters in those diaries, Christine and Tony. Who or whatever they have changed too are strangers to us, we know nothing of their present life, so you write about what you know; confine it to the sixties surely you have enough material to do that." "You mean end the story when Tony leaves London for Australia, Helen thinks that's what he wants."

"Yes, I think you will have to do that. That is the only ending you can use, because we have no idea what happened to Tony after that."
"But if Christine became a successful author, and according to the poem she did, it would be nice to have that in the story and maybe acknowledge Tony's contribution to her becoming successful."
"If she is a successful author Jim, and say Tony does know her name, do you think that he would want the

world to know about their life back then and about his one way love? Maybe that's why he didn't reveal her name; what happened or didn't happen between them in the sixties has nothing to do with who or what she is now, or who or what Tony is. Let's just finish the diaries, see what happens, and take it from there."

"I suppose you have a point there, he was in love with a teenage wannabe, not a middle aged successful author. All right I'll call around in the morning and we'll finish them, maybe he might reveal what happened the night they walked over the heath."

Chapter Eighteen

A damp fog had blown in off the sea overnight, and as I walked towards Ted's every place looked strange and eerie, the road had damp patches where it was covered by a canopy of trees, and the sun was already starting to burn off the fog. An array of spider webs on the furze glistened like Jewells in the odd ray of sunlight. The forecast was that the rest of the day would be very warm.

I arrived at around eleven.
Ted said, "A good morning for blight, luckily I sprayed the spuds yesterday."
"Did the signs of nature tell you that fog was coming in?"
"No Jim, but the weather forecast did."
Ted had a pot of tea made and two mugs on the table which he filled, saying, "Now let us join the company of Christine and Tony once more and try to finish these diaries."

I was reading the evening paper and having a pint in the Swiss Cottage when Ben came in. He said "Good news, we're off to Brighton for the bank holiday weekend."

"Who are we?" I asked.

"We consist of Penny, me and you, if you want to come."

"Penny! You mean the police woman who wanted you to become a guest of her Majesty."

"The very same person, I phoned her up the following week and asked her out to dinner, and she said yes."

"By God Ben you take the biscuit. Aren't they expecting trouble from the Mods and Rockers there for the weekend?"

"That won't trouble us, we can avoid that, now do you want to come or not?"

"I'm not sure, I think Christine is going on a demo, I might go with her."

"Suit yourself, if you'd rather spent the weekend shouting, *Make love, not war,* instead of making love, that's up to you. But surely you must know some young lady who would like to accompany you to Brighton."

"If I go with you I'll travel alone, I'm sure there's an abundance of beautiful young ladies in Brighton. If I was going to Newcastle I wouldn't take a bucket of coal with me, so why take a young lady to Brighton."

"Well bless my old boots mate but you sure are cantankerous these days, anyway are you coming or not."

"How are we travelling, bus or train?"

"We are travelling in style, in my mate Bill's ford Zephyr. He and his trouble and strife are gone to Portugal on holidays, and he didn't want his car on the side of the street for a week; not around his area anyway, so he asked yours truly to look after it."

"All right I'll go with you. I haven't seen the sea since I left home and it would be nice to immerse myself in it once more, when are you going, Saturday morning?"

"No we'll go down Friday evening say around seven avoid the mad rush on Saturday, and I'll pick you up outside the library if that suits you, now I'm off to meet Penny."

"And where are we staying?"

"We are on a caravan site for the weekend; it's more of a mobile home than a caravan, plenty of room for the three of us."

"Okay Ben, I'll see you Friday evening."

We arrived in Brighton at around nine thirty on Friday evening, sussed out the caravan site, unloaded our luggage and went in search of some entertainment.

All the pubs and amusements arcades were packed. Mods on their scooters paraded all around the town. The growl of the Rockers motor bikes seemed to say to the Mods, get out of my way.

Ben said "I can see trouble brewing between them before the weekend is over."

Penny agreed, saying, "It looks like my colleagues here are going to be busy."

I asked Ben, "Any idea where we should go for a drink and some music."

"Plenty of pubs Tony, but which of them have music?"

Penny asked a passing group where we could find some entertainment.

One of them answered, "There's music in the *Norfolk* and the *King and Queens*."

Right Ben said, "Let's try the *Norfolk*."

The pub was packed; we pushed through the crowd to the counter. Ben called for the drinks, a group started to play, first a few Beatle numbers and then Buddy Holly, people were rocking and rolling in front of the band stand.

I noticed that most of the customers were Mods; I shouted at Ben, "We seem to be in a Mods pub."

"That's okay Tony, as long as the Rockers don't pay us a visit."

Ben hadn't the words out of his mouth when a skirmish between Mods and Rockers started at the door of the pub.

Penny Collared one of the barmen collecting glasses.

"Is there another way out of here," she asked him.

218

"For staff only," he said.

She showed him her I. D.

"Follow me," he said.

He led us through the private part of the pub and out on to a side street.

I said, "It looks like we picked the wrong weekend to come to Brighton, by the amount of Mods and Rockers in town this shit is going on everywhere."

Ben said, "Let's go to one of the posh hotels, I'm sure Mods and Rockers won't be allowed in."

"And what makes you think we'll be allowed in."

"Penny can show her I.D to the doorman."

I said, "You go on, I'll wander around to see what's happening, I'll see you back at the caravan park."

I was feeling a bit hungry, so I went in search of a fish and chip shop. You had to be very careful crossing the street as motor bikes and scooters were everywhere trying to outdo each other with wheelies and stunts. I found a fish and chip shop on a quiet side street, it also had a juke box and a small dancing area I ordered rock salmon and chips, with plenty of salt and vinegar.

The waitress, a girl of about twenty with long black hair and tanned complexion asked "if I wanted to take away or eat at the table."

"At the table," I answered.

She said, "Take a seat I'll bring them when they're ready."

I chose a table near the juke box, Gene Pitney's *Twenty four hours from Tulsa* was just finishing. The waitress brought my fish and chips, and then went to the juke box and selected Joe Brown's, *that's what love will do.*

"Nice song," I said.

"It's my favourite at the moment," she answered.

I asked, "How is it so quiet here when the rest of the town is humming?"

"We're a bit off the beaten track for visitors, and the Mods and Rockers are keeping our local customers away, but we've been busy all day, I'm glad of the break."

"Are you working late?"

"If it stays this quiet I hope to finish at eleven, dad will manage, who do you support, the Mods or Rockers?"

"Let's say if I run into a gang of Mods, then I'm a Mod, and if I meet a gang of Rockers, I'm a Rocker."

"Wise, are you from around here?"

"No, I came down from London with a couple of friends, we were in a pub up the town when the Mods and Rockers decided to have a go, it got a bit out of hand, so we got out of there, my mates went to one of the hotels. I decided to explore the town, so I end up here talking to you and listening to Joe Brown, here I said handing her a coin, play Billy's Fury's *half way to Paradise.*

"Your accent's not London?"

"No, I'm from Ireland a place called Waterford, it's on the coast. I've been in London a couple of years now, so I thought I'd visit the seaside and have a swim, looks like I picked the wrong weekend."

"Not really, plenty of quiet places around here off the beaten track to swim at.

"That's okay for a local I said, but how would a stranger find them."

A young couple came in and went to the counter.

"Excuse me, I must serve these people."

"Could you please bring me a coffee when you're ready?"

She served the couple, then came back with two cups of Coffee, handing me one she said, "That's on the house."

"Thanks, would you let me return the favour and buy you a drink when you finish, that's if you know some place where we can avoid trouble; and maybe you could tell me where I can find those off the beaten track places."

"If you walk to the end of this street and turn left there's a nice little pub there, it's called *Ye Olde Shanty* if I finish in time I'll meet you there. The girl working there... Mary, she's a friend of mine and also Irish, we often go swimming together. I'm off in the morning my boyfriend and I are going swimming; we often drive out to a quiet spot away from the day trippers. If Mary is off she might come with us."

"You haven't told me your name."

"It's Maria Del La Cato."

She recognised the surprised look on my face and said, "I was born here in Brighton, my Mother's from here, my father's Italian."

Two more couples came in; she finished her coffee, and said, "If it gets too busy I won't be able to meet you, but it's been nice talking to you."

I walked down the street and found the pub, a nice old fashioned one; I sat on a vacant high stool at the counter, and ordered a light and bitter from a barmaid with an Irish accent, whom I presumed was Mary. I introduced myself saying, "I believe we have something in common."

She said, "And what would that be".

"A friend of yours up in the fish and chip shop, Maria told me you are Irish."

"You met Maria?"

"Yes, she directed me here."

"Yes I'm Irish, I'm from Tipperary, Cahir to be exact, and do you know it?"

"Of course I do, I'm from Waterford myself, on the coast, a few miles from Tramore."

"I know Tramore; my parents often took me there on holidays."

"Have you been over here long?"

"About two months, I'm only here for the summer, trying to put a few pounds together to see me through college."

"What are you studying for?" I asked.

"I'm studying to be a teacher, and what about you, have you been here long."

"Three years now, no work back home. I guess you're one of the lucky ones, a good education and a job waiting for you."

"I suppose I am. It's a shame the way we are scattered around the world to earn a living; do you think it will ever change?"

"We can only hope that someday it will. I guess I came down from London the wrong weekend for a dip in the ocean, although your friend Maria said there's some nice out of the way places."

"Yes down the coast a bit, we often go there."

Mary went to serve some customers I looked around to observe the clientele, a mixture of young and old, some of the old playing dominoes at a quiet table, the young listening to and dancing to the juke box.

I was ordering another pint when I heard Mary say.

"Maria! You got off early."

"I did Mary, I directed someone from your country to this pub earlier on, and I just wanted to make sure he got here."

"Oh he got here alright," she answered.

"Let me get you a drink" I said to Maria.

"I'll have a glass of red wine please, do you mind if I sit she said, pointing at a vacant table, I've been on my feet all day."

I took our drinks to the table, "Now I said about those off the beaten tracks and swimming, you were talking about.

"As I said I am going swimming in the morning, and I hope Mary is of, Mary, Mary "she called, "have you got a minute?"

Mary came from behind the bar to join us, picking up glasses on the way.

Maria asked, "Any chance that you are off in the morning."

"I'm not on duty till three."

"Good, would you like to join James and me in the morning, we're going swimming."

"I'd love to."

"Would you object if this fellow country man of yours

joined us, he came all the way from London for a swim, my I don't even know your name".

"Tony Powell" I answered."

"I have no objection to that Maria, after all we're almost neighbours back home, and I suppose it's my duty to be nice to a neighbour."

"I'll pick you up around eleven in the morning. Now I'll say good night and get to my bed."

"Can I get you another drink before you go," I asked?

"No thanks, it's been a long day."

We said good night to Maria and I asked Mary,

"Have you known her long."

"Yes, we're friends since I started work here, we often go out together, shopping and things, and her boyfriend James is very nice, now I better get back behind that counter before the customers start shouting at me."

I finished my pint, took the empty glass to the counter and said to Mary, "I think I'll have a look around the town to see what's happening."

"Good Night then and I'll see you in the morning."

"Yes sure, I'm looking forward to that, good night now."

It was a beautiful summer night, a full moon shimmered on the surface of the sea, noise from the pier drifted on a slight breeze through the streets. Music, hurdy gurdys, motor bikes and scooters all mingled with the wail of police cars as they sped towards the trouble spots. I looked at my watch, twelve thirty, Penny and Ben would not be back at the caravan site yet, so I decided to walk to the seafront to see what was happening.

The police were involved in running skirmishes on the beach with Mods and Rockers; they were hauling several of them to police vans. Some of the Mods and Rockers had blood on their faces, more had clothes torn off, and the policemen were also bedraggled and cut from their efforts. Christ I thought all this trouble over what music and fashion you like. As the large amount of spectators was hampering the police effort I decided to leave and return to the caravan. Ben and Penny were back, I told them of my night's adventure and that I was looking forward to a swim in some out of the way place in the morning.
Ben said, "I'm sure you are."

I was sitting on the steps of the caravan at about five to eleven when I saw a two door grey Austin A 40 drive into the site, I could see they were searching for a caravan, so guessing it was Maria and Mary, I stood up and waved my towel. The car came towards me and stopped. Maria got out and said, "Good morning, and introduced me to James, saying, "This is my fiancé James Wilcox."

James reached across the passenger seat, shook hands and said, "Glad to meet you climb in."

I got in beside Mary and James drove out of the caravan park.

"How are you this morning?" Mary asked.

"Fine, I didn't have too much to drink last night. When I left the pub I walked down to the seafront to see what was happening."

James said, "Plenty of trouble, I heard it on the radio this morning, it's bad for our image, keeping good honest tourist away, these Mods and Rockers do nothing for Brighton, just gives us a bad name."

I said, "Oh I don't know, ye are getting nationwide coverage, and beyond, you know the old saying *there's no such thing as bad publicity.*

Mary said, "My father phoned the pub this morning to make sure I was alright, said he heard about the trouble on Radio Eireann this morning."

James said, "God Almighty," as he swung the steering wheel to avoid a scooter that shot from a side street on to the main road, the car struck the back wheel flinging it across the road, and then we slammed into a wall on the other side of the road.

The driver's side of the car was against the wall. Mary was moaning and clutching her side, James was slumped over the steering wheel.

I asked Maria "Are you alright."

"I think so."

"Can you open the door?"

She tried to open it, but it wouldn't budge.

"Move forward as far as you can, and bring the seat with you."

I pushed the back of the seat as far as I could into Maria's back, this gave me enough room to pull the handle and give the door a strong kick; it swung open. Maria got out, I followed her.

Other cars had stopped; a woman came from a house and said she had called the police and an ambulance. I could hear the police and ambulance sirens in the distance. Maria was talking to James, but he wasn't answering, I leaned into the back of the car and asked Mary, "Can you get out?"

"I think so."

I caught her hand and helped her out, she raised her jumper, to reveal a cut and bruise on her waist. Some people had gathered around the scooter driver; I went across the road to see how he was, he was unconscious. Two ambulances arrived and two police cars at the same time, one ambulance went to the car, the other to the scooter. The police asked the crowd to move back, a nurse asked me was I alright. I answered yes, and she then checked on Maria and Mary and made them comfortable in the ambulance.

A fire brigade arrived and slowly moved the car away from the wall they then cut the door off the car and removed James and placed him on a stretcher in the ambulance. The other ambulance was already on its way to the hospital with the scooter driver. A police man closed the door and waved it on its way. He said, "I'll drop you home, where do you live?"

I gave him the name of the caravan park.

Ben looked on in amazement as the police car pulled up beside the caravan.

"They finally caught up with you," he said.

Penny came out and spoke to the policeman.

She said. "My God, are you alright?"

"I'm fine."

"And what about the rest of them," she asked.

"In hospital by now, a few cuts and bruises on Mary and Maria, Maria boyfriend James, and the scooter driver are unconscious."

"Will they be alright?" Ben asked.

"I don't know I'll call around to the hospital as soon as I wash of this blood."

"Are you hurt?" Penny asked.

"No it's just dried blood from Mary and Maria."

Penny spoke to the policeman again, and then he drove off.

I washed the blood off and changed my clothes, and said, "I must go to the hospital."

Penny said, "The policeman is coming back, he wants a statement from you, he said he'd drive us there."

When we arrived at the hospital we were allowed in to see James, Maria and Mary were with him looking none the worse for wear. James had regained consciousness, he had some stitches in his forehead and a dislocated shoulder, and they would keep him in for a day or two. The scooter driver suffered a broken leg and was already charged with dangerous driving. Maria said her father was going to collect her later. Mary rode back to the pub with us in the police car.

Penny, Ben and I went to the hotel that they had visited the previous evening, had a skin full, called into Maria's fish and chip shop on the way back to the caravan, Maria wasn't there, the *Ye Olde Shanty* was closed, we ate our fish and chips on the way back to the caravan park.

On my way to the *Ye Old Shanty* at Sunday lunch time I still had to dodge Mods and Rockers; Mary wasn't working, the barman said she would be back on

Wednesday; I had a pint of bitter and went back to the caravan park.

"How is Mary?" Penny asked.
"She's Okay, taking a couple of days off."
Ben said, "Right let's go."
"Where are we going to?" I asked.
"First to a hotel for dinner; then we'll drive out the coast and find one of those out of the way places you were on about and have a swim. We can't let you go back to old Smokey without a dip in the ocean; then we'll go back to the *Ye Old Shanty* for a few pints. I saw a poster in the hotel last night for a dance in the *Kingsland*; it's been a long time since I tripped the light fantastic, so what do you think."
I answered, "I think that's just what the doctor ordered; you never know your luck in a strange town."

^

Ted Took off his glasses rubbed his eyes and laid the diaries on the table.
I said, "I guess he got his swim in Brighton after all Ted, but no luck with Mary."
"Oh yes he had, two weeks later he took the train down on Friday evening, went to see Mary, Maria and James. The Mods and Rockers weren't there, just your average ordinary tourist. They had a wonderful weekend, merry

go rounds, candy floss, dancing, swimming, fish and chips, and pints in the *Ye Olde Shanty*."

"You seem to have no trouble recalling it Ted."

"Why would I? Often Tony spoke of it when we were having a few pints."

"On a weekend such as that he seemed to have no problem putting Christine to the back of his mind and loving other women."

"As I told you before he enjoyed other women, perhaps even fell in love with some of them. But he never loved anyone the way he loved Christine, she didn't love him, so he dealt with that the best way he could.
He didn't isolate himself from women he enjoyed the company of women too much to do that. He didn't become a priest, a monk or a hermit, he didn't become a celibate. He had occasional flings along the way, all of them ended after a short while; he would never tie himself down. He wanted always to be free, just in case some day, some way Christine would love him, if that was to happen he didn't want any obstacles in his way."

"But it wasn't to be Ted, she never fell in love with him, and yet he never fell seriously in love with anyone else."

"I guess he couldn't, he could never feel the same way about anyone as he did about Christine."

"You seem to know quite a bit about the way he felt

232

about her, did he confide in you?

"No, no, of course not, I'm not stating facts, just theory; I'm only assuming that's the way he felt."

"All the girls that he had a relationship with, can you recall their names?"

"It's so long ago, it's impossible to remember all the names, apart from the ones he mentions in the diary, Rebecca the Mayor, Jane in Golders Green, Mary in Brighton and Donna in Hastings."

"Donna was yours Ted."

"Yes, yes, of course she was, I just got a bit mixed up."

"Do you think Ted if one of them called to his door now, and said they wanted to get back with him, do you think that he'd be happy to do so?"

"I don't know; has he got over Christine? Or is he still waiting for her to knock on his door. But he did feel affection for all of those girls, maybe at his age now he'd be glad of the company of any one of them."

"We're nearly at the end Ted, and still no mention of the name Christine writes under, I'm beginning to wonder is Tony Powell having us on about Christine being an author."

"Why? Why should he do that? What would he have to benefit from it?"

"I don't know, without the poem mentioning Christine becoming a famous author, would we have shown the same interest in the diaries. Did Tony think that by insinuating Christine may have become a world famous author, that it would capture our imagination and keep us going to try and find her pen name?"

"Listen to me Jim I know Christine was a poet, I read some of her poems, Tony showed them to me. She was good, very good, and becoming a writer was all she ever wanted; she put everything else on the back burner, including Tony. I don't believe Tony is leading us up the garden path; I believe Christine became a successful author, that she fulfilled her ambition."

"Do you really think that's what she done Ted, put Tony on the back burner? Do you think that she loved him, but decided love would get in her way?"

"I don't know Jim whether she loved him or not. I don't know what she decided, all I know is she was determined to succeed."

"I think he wants to keep where he is, or who he is a secret. And I think Helen is right, the story must finish when he left London; where he went or what he did, or became after that he wants none of that revealed, what's in the diaries must be the basis for the book."

"Come on Jim you're getting paranoid, where he went? He went to Australia, what he became? What do you think he became a spy or something?"

"We can only assume he went to Australia, did anyone we know see him there? And if he did go, how long did he go for? You knew him Ted; you were a friend of his back then, part of the scene, why would he send you a poem and diary without an address; it's a bit of a mystery, unless all is not what it seems."

"Ah God Jim you're really getting carried away, the only mystery we have to solve here is Christine's pen name, if Tony know it, he doesn't want us to know it, as we said before he doesn't want the Christine and Tony of the sixties connected with the present day Tony and Christine, or whatever they are calling themselves."

"I don't know Ted, why would someone not reveal his where abouts to a friend? There must be some reason, why not just send you the diaries and Christine's pen name, and say this is the way it was back then, see if you can get a story from them, and anyway if Christine became a writer, why can't she write the story?"

"Maybe he doesn't know her pen name Jim, or even where she is, maybe they haven't met since he left London, just work with what you know and maybe, just maybe you may get a story or something for your editor."

"I suppose that's all I can do. Anyway one more session will see us through, and I really want to know what kind of conversation Christine and Tony had the night they walked over the heath. Whatever happened that night ended any hope Tony had that Christine would love him. Did Tony meet her that night to tell her he was going to Australia and hope that she would declare her love for him, and persuade him to stay. Or was it whatever Christine said convinced him that she would never love him and triggered Australia in his mind, what do you think Ted?"

"I don't know some of my memories are still a bit dust covered. I'm not sure but I think Tony and Christine had a falling out about a month or so before he left London. Look let's try and finish the diaries tomorrow, maybe they will throw some light on that."
A falling out, what kind of a falling out?"
"I'm not sure Jim; I think something happened between them, whatever it was it seemed to set him on course for Australia. I know he was thinking of Australia for a while, but whatever happened seemed to have made his mind up; I think the walk on the Heath was a walk away walk. You're going back to London on Sunday; you can bring them with you; take your time, and decide whether you got material for your paper, or for a story. You will have to confine your material to what's in the diaries, you have no idea what happened after Tony left

London, and I don't think you should concern yourself about that."

"I don't know Ted, I can speculate, make up something; put my own ending to it."

"No, no Jim, if you stray from the diaries you are talking fiction, maybe fiction would be all right for a book, but I'm sure your editor would prefer a factual story, you said yourself you didn't want to resort to fiction, stay with the diaries. Forget about what became of Christine and Tony, the present Christine and Tony has nothing to with your story; confine your story to the diaries, that's the story."

"We'll see Ted; we'll see. Surely someone must still exist in London who knew Christine and Tony, Ben's family, Ben's friends; surely someone, somewhere.

"Let it go Jim; let it go, if there is a story it's in the diaries."

"We'll see Ted, maybe you're right. Are you going for a pint tonight?"

"I don't think so, I feel a bit tired. All these memories are taking their toll."

"Are you sure you're all right? You seem... your mind seems to be elsewhere."

"I'm grand, it's all this living in the past, I think I need a holiday, catch up with the present; I'll see you in the morning."

At breakfast Helen asked, "Have ye finished the diaries."
"Not yet, today I hope. Is Ted from around here Helen?"
"No, as I told you he came here over twenty years ago, and he's been here ever since. He was away for about a week last year and that's the only time he's been away since he came to live here. I think he went to London because he said to Paul in the pub one night that it only took about an hour from Waterford to Luton compared to years ago when he travelled by boat and train."
"But he is from somewhere here in Waterford."
"I think so, I never asked, he never mentions any other county, so I assume he's from here. Why are you curious about Ted?"

"I don't know, something, a feeling that he knows more than he's telling us; and his insistence that I write only about the Christine and Tony of the past."
"Ah Jim, I'm sure he's telling you everything, sure don't he want the story as well as you."
"I suppose your right, why would he hold anything back? Anyway the diaries are coming to an end, and then it's up to me to get a story or something from them, to justify my week here to my editor."
"Are you going to Ted's this morning?"

"Probably, I hope he's okay; he seemed a bit under the weather last night."

What do you mean?"

"I don't know. It was as if he had something troubling him."

"I hope he's alright Jim, I hope there's nothing wrong health wise."

"Don't worry Helen; it's probably just my imagination, I suppose I better go see him."

"I'm going to the village, so I can drop you off on the way."

Chapter Nineteen

As I got out of the car Ted shouted, "I'm around the back."

Ted was digging some potatoes, a crow on an overhead electric wire was observing proceedings, I said, pointing to the crow, "You have company, probably waiting for you to finish so he can help himself to some".

"Plenty here for all Jim, I always set an extra drill for the crows that was a tradition way back, most people would set what they called, *a crow drill*".

Picking up some and putting them in a bucket, I said "They look good, how are you this morning?"

"I'm grand, no fear of me."

"You seemed a bit down last night."

"Ah no, I'm fine it was all the talk about the past; and all those memories about Christine, Ben, and old friends."

"And Tony, don't forget."

"Yes of course, Tony."

"You knew her well Ted? Christine I mean."

Ted leaning on his garden fork stared into the distance for some seconds, and then said. "Yes... yes, I knew her... I'll dig one more stalk that should do, I promised Biddy Murphy some, then I'll put the kettle on and we'll finish those diaries."

"I had a quick look at the daily paper as Ted was making tea."

Ted said as he came with the tea, "Nothing in there, just bullshit and spin, I don't know why we bother to elect our T Ds; we should elect the advisors and spin doctors instead. No one accepts responsibility."

"I think you're a bit of a cynic Ted."

"Maybe I am Jim, but if the majority of us were a bit more cynical when we vote, we might get a better class of Government, Harry Truman once said *the buck stops here,* we all know where the buck stops in Ireland; in someone's wallet. Now let's enjoy this cup of tea, oh I almost forgot here's the copy of the poem *The Magic Road* I promised you. Now let us transport ourselves via the diaries back to the sixties and enjoy once more the company of Christine and Tony.

I was standing on the footpath as
Christine was locking the bookshop door;
I had a copy of Thomas Hardy's *Far from*
The Madding Crowd in my hand."
"What have you planned for this
evening?" She asked.
 "I'm going to the pub for a pint and then home
to start this book, why do you ask?"

"I'm going to a poetry reading, I and two other
poets are holding a reading in the meeting room
in the library, and would you like to come."
"Me? At a poetry reading! I don't think so.
"Why not, give it a try, you might like it; it will be over at ten."
"I don't know."
"Go on give it a try"
"All right, Thomas Hardy can wait for another evening."
"I've noticed you've picked up a lot of his books."
"I enjoy his stories, maybe it's because I'm from a rural
environment that I can relate to him. He writes about
ordinary events and ordinary people, country life,
farming, farm workers; everyday things. It took the
farmers in Ireland a while to get modernised. They were
still working the farms in Ireland in the forties and fifties
the way they were working them here in England in
Hardy's time, anyway what time and where shall I meet
you?"
"I'll be outside the library at seven thirty."
"Okay, see you then."

The poetry reading finished at ten. I enjoyed it. Christine
read first, then a man in his fifties followed by a fellow
about thirty. Some of the poems I could relate to, others
were beyond me, well at a first reading anyway, maybe
if I had a copy and time to study them they might make
sense. I asked Christine, "Do want to go to the Swiss

cottage for a drink?"

"I'd rather not, but there's a nice coffee shop around the corner and I'd love a coffee, its thirsty work reading poetry."

"Coffee it is then."

Christine sat there sipping her coffee; she seemed a bit preoccupied.

"What's up, you seem to have something on your mind."

"Writing and poetry, I sent some of my poems to a publisher a few weeks ago and I've heard nothing from them."

"It takes time Christine, I'm sure they get hundreds of submissions,"

"Yes I'm sure they do, but I seem to be getting nowhere, and all those rejection slips are a bit depressing, and mother wants me to go to university and make a career for myself."

"That might be wise move as a backup; you could still continue writing, and don't you think it would be good to have something to fall back on."

"I suppose so; anyway let's forget it for now, its nice sitting here talking to you."

"Sitting on a bed of nails would be nice with you Christine."

"Don't Tony, don't go there, and spoil everything."

"Sorry Christine, that's the way I feel."

"We're good friends Tony Just be happy with that for now.

We're going away for a few days."

"And who's we?"

"Mother, father and me, to a book fair in Paris for four days; two days for the book fair and two days to see Paris."

"That's wonderful, Paris in summer, magic."

"Yes but can you manage the book shop, if not we will close it."

"No, no don't close I can manage."

"Are you sure, we could close."

"No, no need, I can manage, when are you going?"

"Tuesday, we're back on Friday, it will be nice to get away from London for a break."

"Couldn't be better, Chelsea are playing Liverpool at the bridge on Saturday. Do you want another coffee?"

"No thanks, I should be going."

"I'll walk with you."

"You don't have to".

"I know but it's a good night for a walk and it will keep me away from the pub."

"Did you ever think about what I said about taking night

classes, that would keep you out of the pub, you're intelligent Tony you could achieve something."

"I've thought about it, I don't know maybe I will, but I was thinking of leaving London."

"What? Leave London, you can't do that, why on earth, you can't do that, where would you go, back to Ireland?"

"No, I was thinking more about Australia."

"Australia? My God, that's at the other side of the world, you can't go there."

"That would definitely keep me out of the pub."

"How would it, they have pubs there as well."

"I know but out in the bush you could be two hundred miles from one."

"God Tony that's a big move. No, no don't go there, go to the night classes and you can have a career here in London; or maybe in Ireland. Australia? No, no, please don't go there."

"Look, don't worry. It's just a thought, maybe by next week I could be enrolled for those night classes, anyway here's your front door. I'll say good night and I'll see you Monday before your adventure in Paris."

"Good night Tony... and thanks."

"Thanks, for what?"

"Thanks for being here, good night."

"Where ever I am in the world... I'll always be here."

Sunday night I was in the Swiss Cottage with Ben and two of our mates, Bill Haney and Pat O Mahony, winding down after a long Saturday night and Sunday morning. Bill hailed from Newcastle and Pat from Dublin. Thanks to Christine and the poetry reading I had no drink on Friday night, but boy did I make up for it last night. So a nice quiet drink was all I wanted tonight. But it didn't turn out that way.

Pat liked a few pints, but Bill's passion was cards, and he would be quite happy to drink water all night, as long as he was playing cards. Bill shouted at the barman for a deck of cards, two lads that Bill and Pat knew asked if they could join us. Bill answered, "The more in the game the more in the pot. Now he said let's settle down to a nice quite game."

I said, "No such thing, I have never yet witnessed a quiet game of cards."

Ben said, "Then we can make history, the first quiet game of cards in the world."

We settled down to a game of poker, it seemed we had just started when the barman was calling closing time.

Bill said, "We can't give up now, not with that pot on the table. Why don't we buy a few cans of beer and go across to my place and continue there."

Bill lived in the flats across from the Swiss Cottage, so we all agreed it was a good idea. Several quart tins of bitter were bought and the game continued until about two o' clock, and then the beer ran out.

Ben said, "It's a pity we haven't a way of going down to Convent Garden, the pubs open early there for the markets."

Bill said, "I haven't been drinking I could drive you down.

I answered, "You'll never fit six of us in that Anglia of yours, maybe five no more."

Ben said, "Maybe one of us could go in the boot."

Pat said, "You must be crazy, what if something ran into the back of it."

Bill answered, "Ah don't be such a spoil sport, now who's going in the boot?"

We all looked at Pat, who happened to be the smallest of us.

"No, no way, I'm not going in that tin can, I want to live to see Anna Livia again."

"Don't insult my car, and who's Anna Livia?"

"Some ould wan he's fond of in Dublin," I answered.

Ben said, "Come on Pat think of the reward at the end of it, a nice creamy pint."

It took another twenty minutes to persuade Pat and then he agreed, saying, "I'll do it but you are not closing the boot, I'll hold it down from the inside."

We all piled into Bill's car and headed for Convent Garden.

Pat raised the boot now and then for a bit of fresh air, and all was going well until we approached Piccadilly, then five or six police cars; their sirens blazing seemed to appear from nowhere.
We were completely surrounded, but they kept their distance and took cover behind their cars.
Then someone with a loud hailer said,"Throw out your weapons and come out with your hands up."
Bill said, "Christ which of ye are carrying a gun."
We all looked at Ben.
"Come off it lads, I haven't seen a gun since I left the army."

I said, "You better get out Bill."
Bill answered, "We better let them know we haven't got any guns, if I step out now they might open fire."
Ben answered, "For God sake Bill this is England, not America, and you've been watching too many gangster films. Leave down the window, and tell them we are all getting out and we haven't any weapons."
Bill said, "Hello! Hello officer, we're getting out; we're not armed."
The loud hailer said, "Come out one at a time and then walk over here."

Bill got out and walked toward the loud hailer when he was a few feet away he was surrounded by police officers and handcuffed.

When we were all out and safely handcuffed the officer with the loud hailer stepped out from behind the car, and said, "Now who's in charge here."

We all looked at Ben.

"Bring him to me, what's your name?"

"Ben Mason, what's all the fuss about?"

"We have a report that you have a body in the boot; a car driving behind you saw a leg hanging out and contacted us."

"Oh! Oh I see, I can explain that."

Just then the boot slowly opened, all guns turned towards the car. Pat climbed slowly out and said, "Are ye's looking for me?"

"Who's that?" The officer asked.

I answered, "Lazarus, back from the dead."

The officer shouted, "Load them up, and the body as well."

We were at least two hours at the police station trying to explain the situation. When at last they let us off, they charged Bill with dangerous driving, being a danger to the public and over loading a vehicle. It was seven o' clock when I fell into bed.

I walked into the bookshop at a quarter to two, Christine was serving someone.

When finished she said; "I see they let you go, what in God's name is the matter with you? On Friday you were either going to Australia or enrolling for evening classes and on Monday morning you are all over the news being arrested in Piccadilly. Were you that much in need of a drink that you had to go to Convent Garden for it at three in the morning? Can I, can we depend on you to be here for the next four days?"

"Of course you can depend on me. I'm here now, and it's only ten to two. I don't start until two, so what's the problem? And I'll be here for the next four days, after that I'm not so sure. Anyway what I do with my spare time is my business."

"I'm just concerned about you, if you want to become a drunk and down and out, well then don't let me stop you."

"Are you concerned about me? Are you sure you know how to be concerned about someone, apart from yourself and your career?"

"That's not fair Tony, you're my friend, and I am concerned about you. But for you friendship is not enough, you want more, right now I can't give you more. I've told you for now my writing is all that matter to me, and you trying to drink yourself to death won't change that. Accept it. I am who I am and getting involved with you or anyone else right now is not on."

"Do you really know what you want Christine, right now you think it's your career, and you are willing to deep freeze any feelings you have for me."
"Don't kid yourself Tony, don't put two and two together and get six, the only feelings I have for you is friendship."
"You're in denial Christine you do feel something for me. You can try to hide it, put it to the back of your mind, but I know it and you know it. From the first day we met in Chelsea something happened between us and you've been in denial ever since, and you can keep on denying it, but it's there and always will be. But remember this, when you think the time has come to defrost those feelings it may be too late, life moves on, we move on."
"Move on if you want to, see if I care. Father and mother have gone shopping and I'm going to do the same, take the key with you this evening when you lock up."

As Christine walked past me I caught her hand and turned her towards me and said; "I love you Christine" and kissed her, when I let her go she walked to the door turned around and said.

"When you finish on Friday put the key in the letter box; if you can't accept us as friends, I don't want to see you again; I'll tell dad you've got a full time job."

I worked the four days and on Friday evening I put the key in the letter box and walked away.

I met Ben and some of the lads in the Swiss Cottage on Friday night; we had a few drinks and a laugh about our escapade in Piccadilly. We went to Stamford Bridge on Saturday for the Chelsea and Liverpool game.

On Monday I went down to Australia house and put into motion my plans for Australia. For the next month I worked on the presses in Fleet Street and did a few door jobs with Ben down west. I got word in the post that I had been accepted for Australia. I gave in my notice at the job and told my land lady that in two weeks I would be moving on.

Ben said, "I don't believe it, as we sat in the Swiss Cottage having a pint, you? Going to Australia! What in God's name do you want to go there for? And when are you going?"

"In two weeks time, I'm going home to Ireland next week, then it's back here and then I'm off."

"God Tony you're crazy, why would anyone want to leave London. You've heard the saying *if you're tired of London you're tired of living* or something like that, you're not tired of living Tony, are you?"

"No Ben, no worries there, I still got a whole lot of living to do, I just want a change; get away from the booze for a while."

"Are you sure that's the only reason you're going; would a certain lady have anything to do with it."
"No Ben, Just the booze."
Yeah sure I believe you! And I also believe in the tooth fair, but there's plenty of booze there as well as here."
"Not where I'm going, two hundred miles from the nearest town, they fly us in there every six weeks for B and B."
"What? Fly you two hundred miles, for bed and breakfast."
"No Ben, not just for bed and breakfast, beer and botty also included."
"Christ mate you'll go mad, nothing for six weeks only sheep."
"Think of the money I'll save.
"Money's not everything, couldn't you feck up to Liverpool or Manchester, wouldn't that be far enough way, Christ mate Australia! It will take you four or five weeks to get there."
"I know, but my mind is made up, I'm going."
"I know you are, we'll miss you, and we've had some good times together, and if you're ever back this way,

look us up."

"Nothing surer Ben, you'll be the first person I'll call on."

Two days before I was leaving for Ireland I decided to go for a walk just to pass an hour or two. In the square across from the railway bar a crowd was gathered around someone singing. I walked over to listen, it was Christine. I hadn't seen her since we had that bit of a barny. When she finished her song some people threw some money in to a cap she had on the ground. I clapped and said, "Beautiful, both the song and the singer.

"Tony? It's you!"

"The one and only me," I answered.

"It's great to see you, where have you been? Why didn't you call to the shop?"

"You made it quite clear, friendship only; or else stay away."

"I didn't mean that. I was just confused; when you kissed me I, I didn't know how to react, didn't know what to do, so I went on the defensive. When you didn't turn up at the shop and I told father what I had said to you, he was as mad as hell. I'm sorry I said I don't want to see you anymore, it was childish of me, and of course I want to see you."

"I'm sorry Christine. I shouldn't have kissed you, but I couldn't resist it, but I suppose you could say I'm leading two nil."

"What do you mean?"

"Two kisses from me to you, none from you to me. Christine you were right about what happened in Piccadilly, it never should have happened, I should have had more sense."

"I suppose Tony you could tell me to mind my own business. I have no right to tell you how to lead your life, but I would hate to see you waste that life on drink, you can be someone."

"I am someone Christine, I'm me, and I can't do anything about that or the way I feel about you..."

Don't Tony..."

"What I'm saying Christine is there are some things I can't change and some things I can, and will. Can you stop busking for a while and join me for a coffee; I have something to tell you."

"I'd love to join you and as a matter of fact I have something to tell you."

I held Christine's guitar as she picked up her cap and money, then we crossed the street to the cafe.

I ordered two coffees and two doughnuts, we got a window table.

"You said you're leading two nil Tony, maybe, maybe someday I might draw level. But right now I, I can't, I'm sorry Tony."

"Not to worry, that's the way it is, and I have to accept it."

"What have you to tell me?"

"I'm leaving."

"What? Leaving London! No, no, you, you can't. I, I don't want you to. Where are you going to, back to Ireland? No Tony you can't leave."

"No Christine, I'm not going to Ireland; well yes, for a week, and then Australia."

"Australia! No, no Tony, you can't go there, it's so far away, and I may never see you again."

"That may be, but I'm going and if we are to meet again, then we'll meet; if not, so be it."

"You can't go Tony, why? Why are you going?"

"I think you know why I'm going, I love you Christine, and you don't love me and probably never will, you . . ."

"No, no Tony, don't go, please don't go. I need time, give me more time, in the future, who knows?"

"You may fall in love in the future, but as your father pointed out there's no guarantee it will be with me. I just can't stay here in London, it's tearing me apart. And the thought that maybe someday we may meet on

some street and you hand in hand with someone else. I
don't want to see that, I couldn't take that."

"But, but that may never happen, can't you stay here in
London and get on with your life, and I'll get on with
mine and let's wait and see what happens."
"I can't do that, I wish I could, but I can't. I'm not the
kind of guy that if I met you with someone else, that I
could walk up to both of you and wish you everlasting
happiness. I couldn't do that, I'd probably more likely
kick the crap out of him."
"Please Tony, please."
"My mind's made up Christine I'm going; now you said
you had something to tell me."

"Yes I have, but I guess it doesn't matter now, come on
its very stuffy in here let's go for a walk on the heath."
It was a really warm summers evening, a lot of people
sitting on the grass.
Christine said, "Let's sit and rest for a while".
She sat down and then stretched on the grass, her eyes
closed, her hair spread on the grass among the daisies,
the sun on her face, and she looked a picture of peace
and perfection.
I thought, if only I had a camera, and then I asked
myself, do I need a camera, this image of Christine's
face; the daisies and the grass will be forever etched in

my mind.

She said, "This is wonderful it would be lovely just to come here every day, and just walk the heath, lay here forever without a care, observe nature and let the world go about its business."

"Yes that would be nice Christine, but that's not you, you want to make the world a better place, not watch it go by."

She got up and said, "Let's walk over the heath to Highgate."

We walked to Highgate Village, on the way we visited the grave of Karl Marx in the old Victorian and then on to the Gatehouse Inn, I called for a pint of ale and asked Christine what she would like.

"A gin and tonic," she answered.

"You're going to take an alcoholic drink?"

"It's not my first time Tony, just because I don't drink it all the time doesn't stop me from having one if I want one, and right now I want one."

It was late when we left the pub, we walked back to the Heath and sat on a park bench, the night was very humid and sultry,

I asked, "What was it that you wanted to tell me earlier on?"

"Oh I don't think it really matters now, not to you

anyway, it's about my writing."

"What about it?"

"I'm going to give it up."

"Give it up, are you crazy? You can't give it up, it means the world to you, and it's what you are. You can't be anything else. You're a writer, a natural, end of story."

"I thought I was a writer, now I'm having doubts; all those rejection slips, they're getting to me, depressing me."

"Listen Christine you're a writer and never mind those rejection slips, they're just the opinion of someone working with some publisher. He or she are not writers if they were they would be submitting to publishers, not rejecting submissions. You are a writer, a natural and let no one tell you anything else."

"I don't know Tony, I'm thinking of going to university, get myself a career maybe I should have gone last year and forgotten about this writing business."

"You can go to university, but don't give up on the writing; thousands of people go to university every year you can be part of that. But you are what they are not, a rare individual. You can write prose, poetry, lyrics; compose music you're one of a kind, you will be published, you will be successful."

"Yes, but when?"

"Success doesn't come over night; it just doesn't fall into your lap. You got to work at it, it takes time, but in your case I have no doubt it will come. Christ Christine a couple of months ago writing was everything to you; it was all you wanted in the world, nothing else mattered. Love, friendship, everything else put on hold. You had one goal only, your writing, and now you want to give it up! What nonsense. If you give it up you will regret it for the rest of your life, and always on your mind the question, could I have made it? It will nag you, haunt you and torment you day and night. You can't give it up and I think you know you can't, it's what you are."

"I don't know Tony; each rejection slip is eating away at my confidence, putting doubts in my mind. And I think maybe they're right; maybe I'm just not good enough to be published."
"How many times have you read in some paper about someone having a best seller after being rejected various times by various publishers? You must keep trying and if you eventually succeed in getting some publishing house to accept you; that alone won't make you successful. The public will be the judge of that, and you must not give up until the public have the opportunity to judge you, you cannot give up."
"I don't know, maybe I'll keep trying."
"You have to Christine, you're a born writer and I mean

literally. You didn't go to some career guidance teacher at fifteen or sixteen and say, I want to be a writer. You are a writer, always were and always will be.

It's in your genes. You are not a teacher, doctor, factory worker; stripper, lap dancer, porn star or business woman. You are what you are and you can be nothing else. You can deny it, you can put it on hold; but it will always be smouldering inside of you, always looking for a way out, accept it Christine. Promise me you will keep trying."

"All right I will, but please, please, will you change your mind about Australia; stay here in London?"

"No I can't, my mind is made up."

"If I said I loved you; would you stay?"

"No, but if you loved me I would. Now come on dawn is breaking, your parents will be worried about you."

I walked Christine to her door and said good bye.

As I walked away I said, "Look after yourself, I'll keep an eye out for your name in the book reviews."

"Tony, do you think we'll meet again?"

"I don't know Christine, who knows what the future holds for us. If we are to meet again, we'll meet."

I went home to bed and slept until around twelve then washed and shaved and went out for breakfast, then back to pack my case and all was ready for my departure.

I went to the Swiss Cottage later, and had a few pints with Ben and a few mates, then we said our goodbyes and I was back in bed at ten.

I was boarding the train from Paddington to Fishguard, when I heard Christine shout my name. I stepped back on to the platform.

"I just had to see you before you left. Why? Why does it have it to be this way? Why can't you stay? Please, please stay. Let's be friends for now and, and who knows? Maybe, maybe in the future. . ."

I'd love to stay Christine, but I can't.

Christine then kissed me, now she said, "It's two to one."

The conductor blew his whistle.

I answered, "I know; but the ref has blown the final whistle, the game is over." I stepped on to the train and said, "Good bye Christine."

∧

Ted left the diaries on the table and sat there in silence.

"Are you alright Ted?"

"Yes, yes I'm fine Jim, it's... my memories; they're not so dust covered anymore... maybe I never should have disturbed the dust."

"God almighty Ted, what was the matter with him, what

a way to say good bye, *the ref has blown the final whistle, the game is over, good bye Christine.* Christ Almighty how anyone could say good bye like that; couldn't he see that she wanted him to stay. What did he want her to do, go down on her knees?"

"Of course not, he wanted her to love him and she didn't. I'm sure he was tempted to stay, that's why he left the way he did. If he didn't get on that train then, he might never have got on it."

"But did he have to get on it; couldn't he have waited, a month, a year? See what the outcome would be, give her a chance."

"I think he knew what the outcome would be; they had known each other for quite a while, long enough for any feelings to develop. I think he had accepted that Christine would never love him. He had two choices; follow Christine around London like a lap dog, or walk away and get on with his life. He chose to walk away."

"But did he get on with his life?"

"I'm sure he did, in some way. Anyway as far as you and I are concerned that's the end, it's over, the end of the diaries. And now the question is can you get a story or something for your editor from it all?"

"I'll try but it's disappointing we didn't find out what name Christine is writing under."

"I know it is; but she hadn't been published when the diary ends, and if Tony does know her name, he chooses not to give it to us. Finish your story, as the train leaves Paddington station, that's the end. So base your story on what's in the diaries. Whatever happened after that? Is a story for another time? You take the diaries with you; you will need them if you are going to write something. Will I see you tomorrow?"

"I'm going back to London early in the morning; I may not get a chance. Are you sure you're okay, I can stay a bit longer if you like."

"No, no I'm fine: it's just, well remembering those times. Christine, the past; I wonder should we let it stay in the past, does it do any good recalling it?"

"It's there Ted, it exists, and it is part of what we are."

"I suppose you're right, do you want a drink before you go? Whisky, beer, tea. . .

"No nothing Ted, I'll be off, do you want to go for a drink tonight?"

"No I don't think so; I'll have an early night."

"All right I'll say goodbye then, I'll keep in touch."

"Thanks Jim, for being here and listening to the diaries."

As I closed Ted's gate, I could see him standing at the window, staring into the distance.

Over dinner Helen said, "You've finished the diaries, any surprising revelations?"

"The only surprising thing was the way Tony said goodbye. But no news of Christine's pen name. Ted seems a bit upset and sad, and I noticed at our last session he seemed a bit upset as well."

Paul asked, "Why he should be upset? The diaries are mostly about Christine and Tony, Ted only gets one mention, the skinny dipping episode with Donna."

Helen said, "He is getting on Paul, and the diaries took him back to his youth and the people he knew then. They are all gone now, dead or scattered around the world, he is bound to be upset about it all."

I said, "He was okay at the beginning very enthusiastic but coming near the end, the last session, and today when the diaries were mostly about Christine and Tony. They seemed to have a greater effect on him. I don't know maybe it's my imagination; he just seemed a bit dejected."

Chapter Twenty

I was two weeks back in London, my editor at the paper said he wanted something in another week. So on a damp Saturday morning I decided to do some work on the diaries which only consisted of deciding where to start. I had the diaries laid out on my table and the note book that I had written some of Ted's observations in. I had not yet decided whether I would try writing a book or just leaving it at an article for my paper, and if I do try writing a book, will I write it as a complete work of fiction, which would give me more scope. But I knew my editor would want a factual story, then I wondered is there any such thing as factual fiction.

I took my coffee over to the window and looked down on the damp street; the clouds were beginning to clear and the sun attempting to shine. I looked at my watch, twelve o' clock and as I was still wondering what name Christine was writing under and Tony and Ted were also on my mind, I decided to walk down to the Swiss Cottage for a pint, just to be in a place that was known to them and hopefully stimulate my mind.

I ordered a light and bitter and a pork pie, and took them outside, the clouds had completely cleared, the sun now shining strong had dried one of the seats that wasn't in the shadow of the pub; I sat down and hoping for inspiration. I observed once again a scene that Christine, Tony and Ted would have observed many times. A tall man I would guess to be around forty came out with a pint and looked at the wet benches.
"This one is dry," I said.

He answered, "Thanks, a bit of fresh air and a pint; that is if there's any such thing as fresh air in London; sometimes I wonder about the smoking ban, especially passive smoking, which is worse? Would I be better off inside inhaling recycled smoke, or out here inhaling recycled petrol and diesel fumes?"
I said, "A good point, though I must admit it's nice to sit out here and watch the world go by."

"I'm not a regular here; I live up Highbury way, an Arsenal supporter. Although my father God rest him was a Chelsea supporter, I won't hold that against him. He was a customer here, and as I was passing I decided to call in. He used to say what you just said, that you could sit here and watch all the nations of the world walk by.
"I'm Jim Clarke."

"Kenneth, Kenneth Mason, my friends call me Ken"
"I've been searching all summer for a man named Ben Mason; it would be a bit of a miracle if you were related to him.

"Miracle or not, that was my father's name, whether it's the same Ben Mason you are searching for... I'm sure they must be quite a few Ben Mason's in London."
"The one I'm talking about was friends with a Ted Patterson..."
"I never heard of a Ted Patterson."
"I knew it was too good to be true, I suppose you never heard of a Tony Powell either."
"I sure have. My father often spoke of him, they were the best of friends, and often he spoke off their escapades together, he came over for my father's funeral last year."

"I'm sorry to hear your father's dead."
"He's twelve months gone now, Mother still misses him, and we all miss him."
"And tell me, would your Mother's name be Penny?"
"It would."
"And, she was a police woman?"
"She sure was; but how do you know all this?"
"You say Tony Powell came over for the funeral last year; came over from where?"

"He came over from Ireland of course; where else would he come from? He returned to Ireland around twenty years ago after some years in Australia and America, and as far as I know he never left it, apart for coming to my father's funeral. What did you say your name was?"

"My name is Jim Clarke."

"How do you know my mother's name, and that she was a policewoman."

"You say Tony Powell is in Ireland."

"He sure is, but how do you know my family?"

"That's a long story Ken, bear with me and I'll tell you, you know if someone said to me yesterday, you can meet anyone of your choice in London tomorrow, I would have picked you. You say Tony Powell was here in London last year for your father's funeral."

"That's right, it was the first time I met him, but my father often mention him. They were great friends many years ago, before he went to Australia."

"And Ted Patterson, he wasn't at the funeral."

"No definitely not, I've told you I never heard of a Ted Patterson, the only people I didn't know at the funeral were Tony Powell and a woman by the name of Christine Arkwright, my mother introduced me to them."

"Christine Arkwright! Was at the funeral?"

"Yes she was, do you know her"

"In a way I know her very well, did they come together?"

"No, I don't think so; mother said that Christine would have only met my father a few times and that would be back in the sixties, she probably came to the funeral knowing that Tony Powell would be there, it seems they were something between them back then."

"Can I get you a pint; you're not in a hurry?"

"No, not in a big hurry and even if I was, I'm not going until you explain everything to me, so I'll have that pint".

"Good, I'm sure you'll be interested in what I'm going to tell you."

"I handed Ken his pint and said it seems Tony Powell kept a diary of what your father and their friends were up to in the sixties. He sent that diary to Ted Patterson, and Ted showed it to me, hoping I can write a story from it."

"That's interesting; and can you get a story out of it?"

"Maybe, but Ted wants the story confined to the sixties, it seems Christine went on to become an author but not under that name, and we don't know the name that she writes under or where she is. Meeting you here was a stroke of luck, what you just told me about Christine and Tony is the first up to date information I've heard about them since I started on the diaries. I'll tell you what I'll give you my address and you can call around some evening next week and I'll show you the diaries. I think it's only right that you see them and give the go ahead for a story considering your father is mentioned in them a lot."

"I'd love to read them, he told me a few yarns about himself and Tony."
And Ted, Ted Patterson, he hung around with them back then. Are you sure he never mentioned him."
"No, no mention of a Ted Patterson."
"And your mother she met Ted? She knew him?"
"No not that I know, if she did know him, she's never mentioned him."

"Did you meet Tony anytime after the funeral?"
"About two days later he called around to see my mother, said he was on his way back to Ireland."
"Was Christine with him?"
"No he was on his own, I'm sure of that because he phoned a taxi to take him to the airport; but after the funeral we had the reception in a club up in the Archway. He travelled in her car to that; I'm sure of that because I was arranging transport to it and Tony said he would travel with Christine."

"I can't figure out how Ted Patterson could tell me of events and stories involving your father and your mother and yet they never heard of him."

"Unless Ted Patterson got to know Tony in later years and he told him."

"No, No I don't think so, when Ted was reading the diaries, and I asked him to clarify things, he did that in a way that only someone involved could do."

"I don't know, maybe my father didn't know Ted Patterson only in passing, it's a long time ago, people forget, maybe if I mention his name to mother it might jog her memory, but I am looking forward to reading those diaries, will you have another pint?"

"No thanks, it's too early in the day, I've got to go."

"Would Tuesday night suit you if I called around to see the diaries?"

"Tuesday will be fine, but I must say I'm still puzzled as to why your father never mentioned Ted Patterson."

"Sorry I can't help you there, maybe as I said, he knew Tony Powell well and was only briefly acquainted with Ted Patterson but I will mention his name to my mother, anyway I'll see you Tuesday night."

"I suppose when I think of it, most of your father's escapades mentioned in the diaries were with Tony Powell, anyway Ken I'll see you Tuesday night, and thanks, you've been a great help"

Ken called around on Tuesday night and he scouted through the parts of the diary that mentioned his father and was delighted with the contents. He had no objection to anything that was in them. He said his mother had come across the name of Ted Patterson in an old address book when she was going through some of his father's things a few weeks after his death."

I said, "So your father did know Ted Patterson, strange that he never mentioned him."

"Maybe like I said, he met him just in passing."

"I don't think so Ken. Ted seemed so well acquainted and knowledgeable with all the events in the diary he had to be involved."

"I don't know Jim, that's the only time mother came across his name."

"Has your mother still got Ted's address in Ireland?"

"No she disposed of all of those things a few months after father's death."

"Has your mother any idea where in Ireland Ted lived?"

"She's not sure, but she thinks it was some place called Waterford."

"Waterford? I wonder...no, no that's ridiculous

"What's ridiculous Jim?"

"Nothing Ken, just a crazy thought flashed through my mind. Are you sure that address your mother found is the one and only reference to Ted Patterson."

"That's the only one, now I must be going, thanks for a look at the diaries and I'll be looking forward to the book."
"I hope I can write it Ken."

After my conversation with Ken, I began to put two and two together and this time I came up with eight, anyway I phoned Paul and told him I had met Ben's son in the Swiss Cottage. "A million to one chance" he said. "Seeing that the population of London is probably over twelve million Paul, it probably was a twelve million to one chance. Tell Ted I met Ben's son and that I'm coming to Ireland on Friday."
"I'll call around to him this evening. Do you want me to collect you at the airport?"

"No thanks Paul I couldn't get a flight to Waterford on Friday so I'm flying into Dublin, I'll hire a car there and drive down, so see you on Friday."
"See ya."

Chapter Twenty One

I left Luton at three thirty on Friday afternoon and
landed in Dublin at four thirty, hired the car and was
knocking on Ted's door at seven o' clock.
No answer from Ted, so I knocked a second time, still no
answer, I walked around to the vegetable garden and
shouted Ted! Ted! My shouting disturbed a magpie that
was perched high up on a tree.
I went back to the car and drove to Helen and Paul's.

Helen was delighted to see me, and asked, "How are
your father and mother?
"Great, they send their regards."
"You're just in time to for a bite to eat, I worry about
young men living on their own, do they eat enough?"
Helen put a plate of mashed potatoes, roast beef,
carrots and gravy in front of me.
She said, "Get that into you and you will have the
strength to tell us what you learned from the person
you met in London.
Ken, Ken Mason, Ben's son. It was some coincidence, he
told me two interesting things, Tony Powell and
Christine Arkwright met last year at Ben's funeral. He
said they were expecting Tony at the funeral, but

Christine was a surprise as she had only met Ben a few times, and that was way back, she had never been in contact with them, Ken thought she only came to meet Tony. And he also told me neither he nor his mother never heard of a Ted Patterson, although his father told him several times about Tony Powell, he never mention Ted. The only time they came across the name of Ted was when Ken's mother was going through Ben's thing a few weeks after he died. On a piece of paper in an old address book they found Ted's name and his address here in Ireland."

Paul said, "He must have known him then."

"He must have Paul, but why never a mention of him to his wife or son, surely when recalling some of his escapades with Tony he would surely mention Ted, and Ben's wife, she knew Tony well, surely she would have met Ted if he was hanging around with them, when reading the diaries Ted gives the impression that he was part and parcel to it all."

"What are you trying to say Jim that Ted wasn't party to it all, that he wasn't there; in London at that time?"

"I don't know Paul, I was hoping Ted could clear things up, that's why I came over."

Helen said, "Well then what are you waiting for? Go around and see him.

"I've already called around, on the way here, he's not

there, any idea where he might be."

"No, no, not really, it's too early for the pub, maybe he's gone for a walk, or around to Biddy's, I'll phone her."

"Hello Biddy, Helen here, listen Jim is back again from England and he was hoping to meet Ted he called around to his place; but he's not there, is he there with you?"

Gone away! Yes, yes, key to his house... and his car, a letter for Jim, yes I'll tell him, we'll call around, in about half an hour, okay bye Biddy."

"What's all that about mother?"

"Ted's gone away, he called into Biddy this morning, said he was going away for a while, and gave her the key to his house, and asked if she would mind lighting a fire in it once or twice a week. He also gave her the keys to his car for Paul, and said he might take it out for a drive now and then."

Gone away? Where in God name is he gone to, and a letter for me? And if he's looking for his car to be started and a fire lit in the house he must be staying away a long time."

"Biddy didn't say Jim."

Paul said,"Let's go around to Biddy's now."

Helen said, "Now, now I'm not leaving all this wash up here, Biddy's not going anywhere. Let's have a cup of tea then wash up, and I'll come around with you, I wouldn't miss it for the world."

Biddy said, "Come in, I'll put the kettle on, and over a cup of tea I'll tell you what I know." No need for tea Biddy we've just had some at Helen's."
"Now Jim, just take it easy, another cup won't do us any harm."
Biddy placed a china teapot covered with a tea cosy in the middle of the table saying, "We'll let it draw for a while," she got four cups and saucers, some biscuits then sat down.
I said, "Now tell us what happened this morning."

"I will, but first let me tell you about Wednesday evening."
"What about Wednesday evening?"
"Well now Jim I'll tell you, I was walking my dog and I was just at Ted's gate when this car stopped and the driver let the window down, a woman it was. She said excuse me, I wonder could you help me, I'm looking for Tony Powell, I think he lives around here some place. Tony Powell I said, now let me think, Tony Powell...Tony Powell, no, no, can't say I ever heard of him, and then I remembered Jim that you mentioned that name at Ted's one morning, so I said go up there and ask Ted, he might be able to help you."

"Thank you she said and got out of the car and walked up to Ted's; can you imagine my surprise when Ted met her half ways up the path and they embraced and kissed."

Helen said "What? Are you telling us that some woman kissed Ted in the middle of his path, in the middle of the afternoon?"

"I am, and he kissed her."

"Was she from around here?"

"You must be joking Helen, who from around here would kiss Ted in the middle of his path in the middle of the afternoon. She was English and she drove an English car, and then this morning that same woman and car stopped outside my house." Biddy took the tea cosy off the teapot and poured four cups of tea.

I said, "For God's sake Biddy never mind the tea and tell us what happened next."

"Ted came in Jim and said he was going away for a few months and would I mind lighting a fire now and then in the house, and would I ask Paul to take his car out for a spin occasionally. Then he handed me a letter and said, "Would you please give this to Jim when he's over again, so that's it, that's all I can tell you."

Helen said, "All this happened Wednesday evening and they called around to you today, where was this woman for the last two nights?"

Biddy said, "All I can say is her car never left Ted's since she parked it there on Wednesday evening, and I'm certain she didn't leave either."

"Well I never, what's the world coming to at all?" Helen asked.

Paul said, "I know who it is; it's Donna... Donna, that's who it is."

"I don't think so Paul."

"Then who is it Jim?"

"I'll tell you, but first let Biddy continue, and she didn't kiss Ted Patterson.

Biddy said, "She did Jim, I saw her, right there in the middle of the path, in the middle of the afternoon."

"Sorry Biddy I know you saw her, but it wasn't Ted Patterson she kissed."

"Jim I know I'm getting old, but my eyesight is still good, and I have known Ted Patterson for over twenty years, and I have no doubt, she kissed him."

Helen said, "Now Jim if Biddy says she kissed Ted, and then she did."

"It wasn't Ted Patterson she kissed... it was Tony Powell, and the woman who kissed him was Christine Arscott."

"Tony Powell? Tony Powell... Christine Arscott? God almighty Jim, are you feeling all right, are you telling me that the two people we've been obsessed with for the last few months, suddenly and like magic materialised out of the blue."

"I know it's hard to believe Paul, but I think it's true."

Helen said, "Listen Jim, Biddy knows Ted; he's been her neighbour for over twenty years and who ever this woman is... if Biddy says she kissed Ted then she did."

"Biddy have you got that letter?"

"I'll get it for you Jim."

Opening the envelope I said, "I hope the contents of this will explain everything."

Hi Jim

I guess by now you have put two and two together and realise that Ted Patterson and Tony Powell are the same person. I must apologise for misleading you, and for not telling the truth at times. I never intended to mislead you but when you showed so much interest in the poem / song and said it would make a good story it got me thinking maybe you were right. And if had to go with you on the story, I knew to conceal my identity I would have no choice but to tell a few fibs along the way and throw in a few red herrings.   I had written the diaries a few years earlier and the night after we discussed a story in the pub when I knew that maybe the poem wasn't going to be enough for you. I decided to dig them out. And on reading them again, I thought maybe in the hands of a writer they could make a story. I made a few adjustments to them, adding my present name Ted Patterson to the sixties scene just to add authenticity to them. The episode with Donna and the mud on Hampstead Heath was Tony, as you've probably guessed by now.

When Paul told me that you had met Ben's son Ken in London I knew that you would put it together, though I must tell you Christine showing up on my doorstep on Wednesday was purely a coincidence and had nothing to do with you meeting Ken. She turned up out of the blue and had to be in Paris by Saturday, the fact that I went with her is the only reason I'm leaving you this letter, otherwise I would be there to meet you and explain everything in person,

Where to start? I suppose in Australia that's when I first morphed into Ted Patterson. I was working in Sydney and had over stayed my welcome, just managing to keep one step ahead of the emigration authorities. I was also playing a bit of football with two different clubs I used my own name for one and Ted Patterson for the other. When I moved up to Cairns and another player from the club where I used the name Ted Patterson moved up there as well, I had no choice but to keep that name, and after a couple of years I managed to wangle a passport in that name.

That's the name I went to America under. Some years later I returned to Ireland still using that name, I wrote to Ben to let him know I was in Ireland and that I was using the name Ted Patterson, any time he wrote to me here he used that name. I had Left Tony Powell behind me many years ago and I suppose if you hadn't met Ken he would still be behind me, maybe not though. When I went to London last year to Ben's funeral I met Christine, our first meeting since I left London, and like me she never married.

She said "I have had great success with my writing, four best sellers, two of them turned into movies; my poems have appeared in magazines and newspapers worldwide, the success I craved and gave you and everything else up for. I've travelled the world I have had several boyfriends and the offer of marriage from many and accepted none, and through it all, always at the back of my mind, you!"
She asked me "do you remember the song Peter Sarstedt sang, where do you go to my lovely when you're alone in your bed. I'll tell you where I go Tony when I'm alone in my bed, or alone anywhere else; back to that book shop in Belsize Park, back to those years

when we were together, we laughed argued, went to demos and generally had a good time and you kissed me twice and wanted to love me forever. But I hadn't time for love, did everything in my power to overcome and subdue it, the only time I came close to realising that I might love you was when I kissed you at Paddington Station the morning you were leaving. Do you know Tony when that train took you away from me that morning; it took some part of me as well?" She asked "do you think it's possible to be in love with someone and not know it". I said "Christine I don't know, and if you don't know by now whether you are in love or not, I guess you never will."

We met the day after for a meal. That's when she gave me her book with the words, "to a friend for the night we walked over the heath" written in it. That was the first time I was sure she had changed her name, she also gave me the poem "Over the Heath," she said those days were often on her mind, so she wrote the poem about them, she pretended she was me when writing it.

She asked me if I remembered the night we walked over the heath. I told her I did. She said "You persuaded me to pursue my writing, and I did. And yet with all the success I've had, sometimes I feel as if I have nothing, and I keep searching for something; something that I

*just can't quite grasp, something elusive, it's like trying
to catch up with my shadow. It's there, it's part of me,
no; more than part of me, it is me because without me
my shadow would not exist. You are my shadow Tony,
and I am your shadow; always with each other, and yet
out of reach. When I read about Ben's death in the local
paper I knew that if you were still in this world you
would come to his funeral, that's why I came, hoping to
meet you".*

*I asked her why? What had she in mind, her answer, "I
just wanted to see you... to meet you again? I, I don't
know, just to talk, to see if, maybe.... I, I must come to a
decision soon, one way or another". I asked a decision
about what? "About us" she answered. I said, "You
made that decision a long time ago."*

*She said, "I know but was it the right decision, I have
achieved everything in life I set out to achieve and yet
there's an emptiness, and something is telling me that
only you can fill that emptiness" So after saying all that
we said good bye and we parted again, it seems she is
as reluctant as ever to admit that she could be in love,
and I haven't heard or seen her since then.*

*Anyway to bring you up to date, much to my surprise
last Wednesday evening Christine walked up my path, I
met her half way; she kissed me and said, "Now it's two*

all, let's take this game into extra time and see what the result will be."   .

I have no idea what the outcome of this extra time will be, but I'm glad Christine made a draw of it and that the game is not yet over; was it you or Paul said, to meet just to say good bye again, I hope not. Again, I'm sorry I cannot be there to meet you, but Christine has to be in Paris for the weekend and we've been apart too long, and at our age now every day counts, so when it came to a decision between Christine and Paris, or meeting you; sorry to say Jim, no contest.

Start writing the book, and maybe the little white lies and red herrings will be all worthwhile and turn you into an author. Christine and I will be back in London for Christmas, we'll meet you there. I will give you her book then and you will know the name she writes under. She has promised to read your manuscript and maybe recommend it to her publishers, she will also make a decision whether to let you reveal her pen name in the book, you always said you would like to know what became of Christine and Tony; now you know, so you might get the ending you wanted; will they live happily ever after? Time will tell. All the best for now Jim and again sorry for misleading you, it just got a bit out of hand.

Paul said, "God Jim I can't believe it, to think that Ted was Tony all the time, and we had no idea."

"I know, but I don't think he meant to mislead us, if I hadn't heard him sing that song and said it would make a story, we would never have heard of the diaries, would never have heard the name Tony Powell. He would still be in Paris now with Christine, and we would still know him as Ted, I wanted a story. To give me that story he had to conceal his true identity. He had no choice; he changed his name to Ted Patterson years ago, everything he did here in Ireland, he did under that name, his work, pension, medical records, everything, so he could not reveal to us his real name."

Biddy was sniffling into a hanky, she said, "I'll put the kettle on and make some more tea.

Helen asked, "Can you still write the story Jim?"

"I think so Helen, why not?"

"If you write it, won't you make people aware of whom Ted really is?"

"Yes, yes of course, I hadn't thought of that."

Paul said; "Change all the names and the location."

"Maybe I need only change Ted's name, nobody around here ever heard of Tony Powell or Christine Arkwright, no need to change the area though."

Helen said, "I think you will have to change the location, if you don't I'm sure people will recognise Ted, it will make no difference what name you give him, how many people are like him around here? None, there's only one Ted."

"Okay I'll change Ted's name and the county, I'll locate it in the south east instead of the south west, and promote it as a work of fiction."

Paul asked, "And what ending are you going to put to it, that they all lived happily ever after?"

"I don't know. Knowing Christine and Ted, sorry Tony, we are not too sure of what will happen. It would be great for them to live happily ever after, but will they?"

Helen said; "I hope they do, they're both in their sixties now, and after missing out on a lifetime together, let's hope whatever years they have remaining, they can spend them with each other."

"Yes that would be nice, let's hope it happens. I'll make a start on the story, by the time I finish it we may know for sure if their future is together or apart. Maybe their twilight years will be their best years, who knows? And roll on Christmas when Christine's pen name will be revealed."

Paul asked, "Do you really think she will reveal it?"

"I do Paul...why not?"